THE HOUSE ON MAYBERRY ROAD

BY

TROY MCCOMBS

World Castle Publishing

TROY McCOMBS

This is a work of fiction. Names, characters, places, and incidents are products of the author's imagination or are used fictitiously and are not to be construed as real. Any resemblance to actual events, locations, organizations, or person, living or dead, is entirely coincidental.

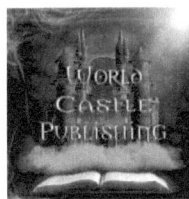

World Castle Publishing
Pensacola, Florida

Copyright © Troy McCombs
ISBN: 9781938961175
First Edition World Castle Publishing July 15, 2011
Second Edition World Castle Publishing September 1, 2012
http://www.worldcastlepublishing.com

Cover: Spittyfish Designs
Editor: Eric R. Johnston

TROY McCOMBS

PROLOGUE

The house on Mayberry Road was nestled deep in the woods, looking oversized and out of place in the wilderness. The house was three stories tall, reaching the height of many of the surrounding trees. Several steps led up to a portico just outside a door with gargoyle knockers and black and red stained glass windows. The clapboard siding looked new, almost as if the house were no more than a month old. The house, which was rumored to date back to before the American Revolution, was still in a pristine state, almost supernaturally so.

Evan White smirked as he gazed at the gargoyles hanging on the door.

"My ass is more haunted than this piece of shit." His voice cracked as he laughed, giving away the fact that he was far more scared than he was letting on. He had brought his girlfriend, Becky Lesko, with him to the "most haunted house in Bellsville" almost as a way to prove himself. After their last fight, this was his last chance to win her over. She seemed to think he was a momma's boy who was too afraid of his own shadow to ever amount to anything.

Becky scoffed. "Your ass is definitely scarier than this place." She followed Evan's gaze to the door and noticed the gargoyle knockers surrounded by the stained glass windows. "Whoever built this place was crazy. But there ain't no ghosts, beau. If you think you're something macho for dragging me out in the middle of the woods, you're nuts."

The night was dark, the moon nowhere in the sky. The only light illuminating the house was the single working head lamp of Evan's Ford Taurus.

He was determined to walk into that house and go up to the attic, where it was rumored vicious ghosts dwelled.

"Well, beau, what are you waiting for?"

He gave Becky an irritated look, which quickly changed to an expression of faux confidence. "I got this, babe."

He walked up the steps, the sound of his footfalls ringing deeply through the thick wood. The gargoyle knockers looked large in his hands as he lifted the ring to knock on the door. He didn't know why he was bothering to knock. Perhaps it was just for the fun of it, or maybe he wanted to see if anyone would actually come to the door. Either way, he felt a compulsion to do so. When he slammed the ring down, it looked as though the whole house came to life.

A few short moments ticked by.

"Evan? What are you doing?"

He initially didn't know what she was referring to, but discovered that for some reason he had pressed his ear against the door, as if listening for someone coming to answer it. And the strange thing was he *did* hear footsteps. They were heavy, as if from a man around two-hundred-fifty pounds wearing heavy boots. His eyes grew wide, and fear struck his spine. He couldn't move.

"Beau…Evan? What is it?"

Without warning, the door flew open, and Evan came face-to-face with a creature beyond imagination. It was green in complexion, with tentacles streaming off its face. It let out a horrid scream, reached out with its long-fingered hands, and pulled him into the house. The door slammed shut, leaving Becky alone in the dim light of the Taurus's headlight.

CHAPTER ONE

John Rollings was sound asleep when his cell phone began ringing and vibrating, filling his peaceful apartment with the unneeded noise of Van Halen's song, "Jump." David Lee Roth shouted out two verses and one chorus in his tuneless monotone before successfully waking him.

John looked over at the trembling Motorola and caught it right before it tumbled over the edge of the stand. He flipped it open. "John Rollings, what the hell do you want?"

At first, there was nothing. Just breathing. He listened closely and thought he heard what sounded like a snake-like voice, *"The master awakens. Come, John...D'kourikai comes."*

But then a tense male voice came through loud and clear, "Mr. Rollings, this is Sheriff Charlie Steera, from Bellsville. Do you think we could meet?"

John rubbed his eyes and yawned. "Yeah, sure, whatever. Just let me get up." *What is this about? Why would a sheriff be calling me?* "Just meet me out on Mayberry Road." He gave the address. "It's a little hard to fin—"

"I can find it," he interrupted, almost dropping the phone. His heart was racing. He had had visions of that house. It was where...Sarah Pouster...the young girl...

"Good, I'll see you there. And, John, bring an iron stomach. You're going to need it."

John Rollings was a thirty-three-year-old navy shipwreck. He had enlisted right out of high school, but was discharged three weeks into basic when he complained about hearing voices and seeing visions of a strange house in a wooded clearing. A navy doctor diagnosed him with paranoid schizophrenia. He felt the diagnosis was bullshit, but he didn't fight it. In fact, the petty officers in the legal department advised he waive his rights to a hearing or he would have a long stay in the separations division—which was almost like a high security prison—while he waited for the verdict, which would most certainly not come down in his favor.

The voices had only increased as time went on. *"Come to us, John. Come hear the call of the master. He is waking. Come."* These voices called to him, taunted him until…Sarah. He hadn't heard them since.

Wearing ugly yellow boxers and a skin-tight T-shirt, he slipped lazily out of bed and went straight for the bathroom. He looked at his reflection in the mirror. His jet-black hair was so shaggy it looked supernatural in itself, like an amorphous, tentacled creature. Stubble coated his cheeks, chin, and neck, but not his upper lip, where it seemed extremely reluctant to grow. His dark brown eyes were half open, their corners stuffed with slivers of crust. Gazing deeply into the looking glass, he whispered, "The voices aren't real. They aren't real. The house is only a dream. There is no…" The foreign-sounding word D'kourikai almost jumped off his lips.

And then something else, something that just flowed out of him like water through a broken levy. *"It's alllll my fault!"* Tears streamed down his face as panic and fear set in. Before he knew it, his fist crashed into the mirror, shattering it in a spider-web of cracks.

Then he looked into the mirror again, searching his face for answers. He didn't move or look away; his eyes burned into the broken reflection, scrutinizing the dark, churning waters of his soul, a soul that seemed as broken as his reflection. The voices, the thoughts, the memories ate away at his sanity. Memories of a young girl who heard the voices too. They had been calling her to that house. That one hidden away from reality on Mayberry Road.

John, what is wrong with me? Why do I hear these voices? Why do we hear these voices? Voices begging them to go to the house on Mayberry Road.

The girl was Sarah Pouster, and she hanged herself a day after seeking John's help. A note was attached to her Hannah Montana shirt: *John, stay away from that house. Whatever you do, don't go there. The word is not suicide. It is self-sacrifice.*

The image of a pale-faced twelve-year-old girl hanging from a rope haunted him.

"Please, God, help me."

***

A beat-up, brown Lincoln Town car cruised along a winding, wooded country hill in the dead of night. John was driving, trying to see through the stark darkness. His brights were just not cutting it. He got some help when he saw the flashing beacons of a police car coming straight at him, making him swerve off to the shoulder of a narrow roadway. The sirens that followed screamed through the night like whistling fireworks. A cruiser flew urgently past him, going back toward town. It had pulled out of Mayberry Road, that hidden road.

John soon flicked on his turn signal and pulled onto

Mayberry Road, the oldest—and most cursed, some would say—road in Chester County. Gravel popped beneath the weight of his vehicle. Trees lined either side of the road, giving him the sense of isolation. In the distance, he could see a variety of high-powered lights burning. They lit the surroundings like a dim sunrise. Rescue vehicles and fire trucks were faintly visible from where he was; there must have been half a dozen of them parked in the clearing just before the house, each with their own flashing lights.

This isn't going to be good.

A long trail of red-burning flares lined the middle of the road. A soft wind twirled the accumulating smoke. As John progressed, his foot barely touching the gas, he could see a team of rescue personnel walking back and forth up in front of the house. Some were carrying equipment boxes, some tools, some just flashlights, but they all looked rather tense.

He sped up, curious to know why half the valley's police force had been summoned to one specific, out-of-the-way location. What were they doing? And how did this pertain to him?

John then slammed on his brakes as an obese police officer stepped out into the road and held out his chubby hand in a *STOP* gesture. His mouth was hanging open, either because he was out of shape or nervous. He looked at John like he wanted to take out his gun and shoot him for being here where he did not belong. Instead, he hurried over to his window.

John rolled it down.

"Go back now!" the officer huffed.

"But I was called to come out—"

Before he could finish, the cop pointed back up the road. "Go back, or I'll throw your ass in jail. There's nothing for you to see here."

"Somebody called me to come out here. Sheriff Charlie Steera?"

The man said nothing. He simply gazed into John's eyes, making him uncomfortable. *What the hell's going on?*

"Sir, I'm going to ask you one last time. Turn your vehicle around and go home." His warm, wheezing breaths brushed against John's face.

"Sir—"

"Burt, it's okay. Let him through." Another cop stepped out of the darkness. This man was a little leaner, a little shorter, with a prominent handlebar mustache and a small, upturned nose. He had serious eyes but gentle-looking cheeks, much like Winston Churchill. "I'll take it from here."

The nervous officer walked away, and the new one approached.

"John Rollings?"

"That's me."

"Hi, I'm Sheriff Charlie Steera. I'm the one who called. Hey, why don't you park right over there by the bushes? Then we'll talk."

John pulled over by a large row of shrubs and put his car in park. He then popped open his door and stepped out onto moist ground.

It had rained on and off for the past few hours; the dull smell in the air declared the possibility of additional precipitation sometime soon. Most of the paramedics and policemen were wearing shiny yellow overcoats, while others weren't wearing any coat whatsoever. They all looked busy, talking secretively to one another, and hiking into or out of a wooded path where *Do Not Cross* police tape had been stripped down...at least for the time being.

John was in awe. He could clearly see the outlines of dozens of trees and their branches silhouetted against the backdrop of powerful tungsten lights set a little farther back in the woods. *Something* back there was all his to explore.

"I really don't know where or how to begin," Steera said, while John looked at the ghostly-lit trees.

Steera leaned in close and said quietly, "The house back here is supposedly haunted. That's what the locals say, anyway."

John turned and looked at the house. This was the house that Sarah had been drawn to, the one that led to her suicide. "This house…" is the source of all those voices, he wanted to say, but couldn't.

"I know. It's gotta be the oldest house still standing in the state, yet structurally, it could have been built yesterday."

"What do you mean?"

"Just look at it. Doesn't it look almost new?"

In fact, it did. The longer they stayed here, the more John felt his heart pound. He could feel the pulsing pounding in his temples. This part of his life had been over, but all those voices, the visions, the psychic mysticism—it was all back, and somehow Charlie knew about the voices and visions.

The question was, how?

"There are stories of pets—dogs and cats—disappearing in these woods and then found mutilated in the street, sometimes hung on signs or nailed to houses. One night, a Bellsville resident swore on Jesus's soul that she saw a light blinking in the woods near that *same* house. Claims the light glowed a certain *color* she claimed wasn't supposed to be visible to the human eye. Have you heard about Oscar Carrin?"

John shook his head.

"Brightest, most athletic kid in town. Star quarterback. Had his head on completely straight. He went into that house on a dare. The boy wasn't in there a minute when, according to his friends, he came out of the place as insane as Charlie Manson. He's locked up in Buckeye Institution now. Doctors can't find out what's wrong with him. But they do say—"

John interrupted: "What I want to know is what happened now, tonight. Why do you have an army of people going in and out of the woods like it's the end of the world?"

Steera took a deep breath. "Hours ago, a girl, Becky Lesko, daughter of one of our deputies, said some kind of creature devoured her boyfriend out there. Evan White was his name. She drove his Taurus to the police station, in total shock…and then, as a unit was dispatched to the place, trails of limbs, organs, and blood led right into these woods." John thought of what Steera had said about dogs and cats.

"It's true, Mr. Rollings. Every word."

John lowered his head. "Sheriff, you've got a serial killer on your hands. Possibly even some wild animal. Definitely nothing supernatural." But he didn't believe it any more than he believed Madonna was really a virgin.

Steera's serious-looking eyes looked one notch more serious. Mean, even. "What I saw that was left of that young man, no animal or psychopath could do. And what can make a sixteen-year-old's hair turn from black to milk white?"

John rubbed his chin, thinking. "It could be a few different things."

The Sheriff grew eerily quiet. "I know this town. I've lived here all my life, and have been sheriff the past twenty years, and the only thing that's ever been out of place is that house. It's cursed. Demonic. Evil."

The sheriff sighed and now shook his own head. John didn't look away from him. Meanwhile, an EMT walked by, carrying a large clear plastic bag with something bloody, slimy, and brown inside. "What is that?" John asked. The EMT snorted. "The kid's liver."

Steera put his hand on John's shoulder. "There's still a lot you don't know yet, John. You see, two of my men went into the house not hours ago, and do you know where they went?"

John shook his head. As he did, a soft breeze blew past, brushing his hair away from his forehead.

Steera looked him dead-cold in his eyes and said, *"Neither do I.*

"They never came out. The second went in with a radio and we can't get any signal from him. Now, whether this is some kind of supernatural—whatever you want to call it— *event,* or a serial killer, we can't say, but I know you know about this house, John."

How do you know that? Was it because of Sarah?

The two men gazed up at the building, Steera with slight fear, John with no emotion at all.

"We've checked for—" Steera stopped, realizing that John was no longer listening to him. "What are you doing?" John had two fingers to each temple, his eyes shut. He took long breath after breath after breath, as if he were in pain.

Then he opened his eyes and looked toward the house.

More Chester County personnel scampered around as John left Charlie's side and walked forward, straight toward the front door. The mud beneath his tennis shoes squashed and sucked him down every time he set foot into it, making him walk like a scuba-diver with flippers. A few drops of rainwater fell softly against his pale face.

Large amounts of blood saturated the ground in front of the porch. It was the most he'd ever seen in his life. There were still chunks of meat mixed in with it, waiting to be whisked away by Steera's men.

As John drew closer to the house, the rescue crew began to gawk at him. One stepped away from a window and shook his head; another dropped his mouth open and widened his eyes; another crossed himself.

He was frightened, but he continued forward, getting closer and closer to the small front porch.

"He's not going in there, is he?" a nearby man in a lab suit whispered.

"Jesus God!"

"Wait! Sir!" A young police officer stepped forward to prevent John from going any farther.

Charlie stopped the nervous rookie from inhibiting John's progress.

John slowly and cautiously walked up the remaining steps. The porch he stepped onto looked homey enough. The windows on opposite sides of him were in near-immaculate condition and were impossible to see through from this angle or this time of night. The door ahead was slightly ajar; the gargoyle knockers stared back at him with their vicious grins. Still, there was no evidence in John's mind that this abode was in any way infested.

But when he reached for the knob, he stopped and looked back. Every man and woman standing in the clearing—*all* of them—had stopped what they were doing to watch him. Over twenty pairs of eyes were waiting to see him disappear from the face of the planet, to be taken alive by whatever demons supposedly infested this place.

"You know we're here, John. We're here and waiting."

John grabbed the knob, opened the door, and entered.

The inside was nothing like the outside. The air smelled of rancid meat and a plethora of other smells impossible to identify. Despite the massive lights blazing through the clearing outside, the inside was a few degrees above pitch black. The windows were neither tinted nor covered with drapes, but somehow blocked any light from coming in from outside. He felt suddenly drawn to this house despite the darkness. It was an overwhelming emotion he had never felt before, not in *any* previous house. He could not begin to understand it.

He reached out and felt his way farther into the room. Luckily, there was nothing in the way, nothing for him to trip over—just a wicked smell as potent as vinegar. It burned and felt cold all at once, quickly filling up his airways. He couldn't breathe. He tried to retreat, but as he turned, the door slammed shut with a loud *BAM!*

He fell to the floor as he struggled to breathe. *"You'll love it here, John. Your soul is mine,"* a voice spoke in his mind. *"Come join me."* He fumbled around, feeling for anything that could serve as a weapon, or an instrument that could break open the windows.

But then he heard the loud thud of footfalls. His hand shot out and grabbed onto something hard, slimy and round lying on the floor. It was a bloody bone attached to the skinless corpse of a large male.

"John! John, answer me! John!" Steera's voice, filled with urgency. He and his men were trying to break down the door from outside.

***

"John? John?" It was a meek man's voice, faint and distorted. There was no urgency in his tone, only softness. Consciousness slowly floated back him as he lay on a hospital bed. John opened his eyes. In his blurred vision, he saw the silhouette of a male figure standing over him.

"What the..." John tried to sit up.

The doctor, an older man with bronze-colored skin, laid a hand on his chest.

"Easy there, pal. Don't move fast or hard just yet."

John lay still, trying to remember what had happened. "You scared us," the doctor told him, checking his heartbeat with a Stethoscope.

"I couldn't breathe..." John took a pan of his surroundings. He was in a hospital. The doctor smiled. "You were choking when they brought you in. It's what was in your lungs that interests me."

John began to sit up again. The doctor helped him. "What was it?"

The doctor sighed, "Lord only knows. When they rushed you in here, you were foaming at the mouth and in spasms. Your eyes were open, but you weren't conscious."

"What was I choking on?"

"Whatever it was, it turned into a pink gas before we started to pump it out of your system. It was in your airways, your stomach, and had somehow gotten its way into your nervous system. The thing is, one of the paramedics said that the fluid you were coughing up in the ambulance was burning holes through the metal floor and gurney bars. Five light bulbs in your ER room burst when this stuff changed from liquid to vapor. I've never seen anything like it."

"Am I okay to go?"

"Yes, you're okay to go, but I would like to do some more tests on you, just to see if there's any trace of the chemical compound still in your body. Urine samples, blood samples, the works."

Without responding—without knowing how to respond—John got up and left.

"You're alive!" Charlie's loud, fascinated voice startled John as he entered the hospital hallway. The sheriff was standing against the wall by a vending machine, visibly exhausted from a sleepless night. His face was pale and dark circles dangled under his blood-shot eyes.

John immediately halted and turned. "Christ, Steera, what happened?"

"Isn't that the question of the day? I would really like to know, myself. We found you clutching onto human remains. When we found you, we thought it was you screaming, but it wasn't. Not really. I don't know. Something was screaming your name. Demanding your soul."

John felt dizzy, stumbled, and reached for a wall. Steera quickly grabbed him, stopping his fall just in time.

"Take me home, please," John said.

CHAPTER TWO

It was midnight before John turned off his bedside lamp. He was sitting straight-up in bed, meditating. The house...that house. The voice in his head calling for him to join him. The darkness surrounded him, embraced him. Random thoughts and voices came, invaded, then drifted away as quickly as they had come.

The house flashed inside his mind. He gritted his teeth. The pain in his head was instantaneous. His fingers twitched. All concentration was lost. He opened his eyes to nothing but darkness.

***

Early the next morning, John hurried out through the doors of a local Starbucks, a steaming cup of coffee in one hand, a cell phone held up to his ear in the other. "Hello? Sedree Harsol?"

"'Ello?" the voice on the other end was far from American.

"This is John Rollings. I'm the one who—" John marched down the sidewalk, passing by store after store.

"Why are you calling me?"

"I entered the house last night." John finagled his way through a swarm of teenagers coming from the opposite direction. "You mean in a dream? You dreamt of the house?"

"No, no. I—I actually went *in* it." John buzzed past an old woman with ugly white hair.

"And you survived. Not possible." Sedree was interested, although it was clear to John that this man didn't believe him. Sedree Harsol was his shrink, the man who helped him when he was nearing suicide. He warned him to stay away from that house because of its associate with the Pouster girl. John told him the whole story in vivid detail by the time he got to the end of the block. Once he got there, he stopped, took a sip of coffee, and recoiled. Still too hot.

"I'm happy you're still with us, John, but you…are you going to be all right?" This time, the old man coughed hoarsely.

"I'll be fine. I'm heading to a library now to see what I can find out about this place. Check its history, see what files come up. I know this may not be anything you're familiar with, but have you any idea what I might be dealing with?" John quickened his pace as he crossed the street.

"Forgive me, but I'm certain it's all in your head. The voices have manifested themselves into a physical form that is haunting you. By no means would I say what happened to you in that house was *real*. But—"

"What about Sarah? She went in that house and then killed herself. And what about the kid from last night, the officers?"

"John, Sarah was a sick child. Depressed. There is nothing supernatural about a teenager hanging herself."

"How do you explain—"

"Humans have been killing humans since the beginning of time."

"A serial killer?" John took a sip of coffee.

"Perhaps."

"All right, then, well, I'll just get Steera on that."

"John, what is your affiliation with the police anyway? Why is Steera seeking your assistance?"

"I-I don't know. I…" he trailed off. For whatever reason, it hadn't occurred to him just how strange it was that the Chester County sheriff would call him, of all people, for help on a case…unless, "Unless he knew I had some connection to the house. Maybe he saw something about Sarah in the paper and thought maybe I knew something." Harsol offered no speculation.

John hung up the phone, disappointed.

The sidewalk cleared out quickly. The streets, too, were empty—a bleak reminiscence of a lively asphalt paradise. A few horns honked in the distance, just loud enough to let John know the world was still alive. John walked casually, drinking his coffee, approaching the alley up ahead, where he could take a shorter route to the Bellsville Library.

He suddenly felt eyes on his back, gazing at him, watching him closely, but when he turned, nobody was there, not on his side or the opposite side of the street. In fact, it was so deserted that he thought something was wrong. A chilly wind brushed back his bangs and shook the overhanging traffic light, whose red STOP signal stayed permanently in place.

Without really thinking, John turned and hurried down the narrow alleyway, wanting to find a more populated area.

Airborne newspapers brushed off the cobblestone pavement, tumbling away in a chilly breeze. The cracked walls on either side of him displayed recent ugly graffiti done by the town's local troublemakers. Crates and garbage-filled boxes littered parts of the walkway, as did broken hypodermic syringes.

He turned. Something was there, following him. Standing

ten yards away was the largest, dirtiest Doberman Pinscher he had ever seen, its jaws open and oozing saliva. Its panting breaths drowned out the sound of the wind and the sound of the bottle rolling slowly toward his feet. The animal growled viciously. Its black eyes gazed directly into his, waiting for him to make the first move.

"Easy, doggie..." he said.

The dog stepped forward, growling louder, its nose scrunched in a snarl.

"Shit, shit, shit," he said, taking three steps backward. As he did, it was already too late. The predator pounced, running at him so quickly he barely had a chance to blink or draw in a breath.

But to his surprise, the dog jumped past him.

Turning, he saw the canine holding a street thug's arm in its sizable jaw. The thug was holding a metal pipe as if he were intending to brain John with it and possibly steal whatever money he could from him. The pipe hit the concrete with a distinct *p-tink*. The man turned and fled, bleeding. The dog chased him for a moment, then stopped and came back to John and lay down at his feet.

John knelt down to pet his canine savior, absorbing what had just happened. Air came back into his lungs. His mind calmed. His wits returned.

He recoiled when he felt the warm, wet snout of the dog brush against the back of his neck. It whimpered and whined, and then licked the side of his cheek. "Thank you. Now I owe you one. What's your name, pal?" he said, searching for a dog tag, but found none. Probably a stray. A lot of people in Bellsville turned animals loose.

He stood back up before he got too attached. The animal squatted down, its tail wagging.

"I'm sorry, but you can't go with me. Really. It's not

going to happen."

The dog rose off the ground and barked.

John shook his head and took a step away. "No! Stay put! You'll find a better owner. I can barely take care of myself." He backed away, finding himself unable to break eye contact with the poor animal, who began whimpering like an abandoned child. When it finally cocked its head to the side, dispirited, John had had enough. He turned and jogged away, about to shed tears of his own.

**

He entered the library ten minutes and two blocks later, his mind more focused on the dog than the house on Mayberry Road. The Bellsville Library, the smallest one in the area—maybe the world—was the only place to do any real tangible research. There were a mere fourteen aisles cluttered with old books that made the building smell like an old folks' home. Three study tables, none of which were occupied now, formed a triangle near the middle of the room. One lone computer occupied the far corner, adjacent to the rear exit door.

"Hello." The two unified voices came from behind a counter. Faint, meek, and female. The librarians, two old women, barely five feet tall, welcomed him with smiles. They looked like identical twins.

"May I help you with something, sir?" the closer one asked as she stamped a book.

"Yes, I need to look through any old files, microfilm, or the internet concerning a house in town here."

"What, you a real estate agent?" she said with a repulsively fake smile.

"No, uh, I'm helping the police research events surrounding the house on Mayberry Road."

"You're a cop?"

"Well, not exactly…I guess you could call me a private investigator. Sheriff Steera thinks I'm qualified, so I guess that works for the county, and works for me too."

Both women were noticeably unnerved. Something clearly frightened them about the request. He smiled, trying to alleviate the tension in their unified looks.

"Don't they have that house off limits? Haven't they yet learned anything from its history? Don't you know why we tried to bury it in the forest? To hide it? It just won't go away." The woman paused. "The Prestillions were *evil!*"

"They were the original owners?"

"Yes. Craziest story I ever heard. Craziest because almost everything anyone's heard about it is true." The woman's face puckered up. New wrinkles formed. Her bottom lip quivered.

"Okay," John said. "I'll leave you two alone. I think I can find what I'm looking for on my own. I'm just going to get on the computer."

When he sat down at a computer, he typed into Google "Strange events in Chester County. Mayberry Road. The Prestillion's House" and hit ENTER.

He clicked the first link that appeared.

The headline read:

"The Chartonsburg Review–1796—Local Renowned Scientist, Charles Prestillion, Builds New House On Mayberry Road. A resident of Chester County since 1774, Charles W. Prestillion has won prestigious awards all around the country for his research in Botany, Biology, Chemistry, and Advanced Mathematics. His recent accomplishment was helping construct his brand new Colonial last May. He lives there now with his wife, Martha, and his daughter, Sandra, and soon plans to run for office...."

John scrolled down and stopped. Under the text was a drawing of a tall, lean man with a protruding chin and sharp, piercing eyes, and dressed in a suit. He was holding the hand of a little girl, whom, John presumed, was his daughter. She was grinning with all her teeth, and was squeezing a teddy bear under one arm. It was an amazingly lifelike drawing, almost as detailed as a photograph.

He scrolled down and saw:

"The Chartonsburg Review—1800—A Tragedy in Chester County -- Charles Prestillion, age 63, a brilliant man with big dreams, suffered huge loss on Tuesday, after his wife and daughter were found dead in his home. The cause is yet unknown."

John scrolled farther down. Under this text was another drawing of Charles Prestillion, sitting again in a chair and looking completely different from his other one. Here, his face was drained of life, his eyes wild and uncertain, his posture tense and broken. It didn't even look like the same man. He appeared delirious.

John noticed a word cut off at the bottom of the page that caught his interest: *Sus—*

He scrolled down more.

—pected Man, Charles Prestillion, Gone Missing After Failing To Appear In Court On Allegations Of Murdering Family

"While local authorities searched the Prestillion House, one officer was found dead in the attic. Cause of death, unknown. However, sources say the examiner found a strange compound lying underneath the subcutaneous tissue of his dermis. He stated some of it turned into a pink gas upon contact with the air. Results of the source are yet to be determined."

"Friday—The Herald Star Review—1801
"On All Hallow's Eve, neighbors on Mayberry Road

complained of hearing loud, obnoxious noises coming from the woods near the vacant Prestillion Home. One source claims he heard the crying of a young girl. Another claims he heard what sounded like a 'rumbling roar' followed by the laughter of some animal. An elderly woman, who was standing outside at the time, said she began to hear a specific and unfamiliar 'word' spoken by an unseen source. Afterward, she lost her hearing."

John scrolled down some more.

"Sunday—The Herald Star Review—1825

"A Young Boy Blinded

"Late afternoon, on December 5th, on Mayberry Road in Bellsville, fourteen-year-old Robert Silca, armed with his musket, ventured into the woods for a day of hunting. After an hour of maintaining position without spotting a deer, he decided to move to a different location. As he did, he began to get an eerie premonition that someone or something was watching him. It didn't matter how far or fast he seemed to go, he felt that he was undoubtedly being followed. Later, he walked into a clearing, right where the Prestillion house was located. "I didn't feel like it was a house, but rather a large hotel filled from corner to corner with evil persons. Robert claims then that he noticed a plethora of closely-connected, beady eyes staring at him through the top, northeast window. For moments, he couldn't move, as if whatever was watching him had incapacitated his body. He wanted to run, but his legs wouldn't budge. Almost every part of his body seized up. "I could not look away. I had to look and, as I did, my own eyes burned like fire. That's when he says the front door creaked open by itself, as if the house was inviting him in. The boy aimed his musket, wanting to protect himself, but was terribly afraid to fire in case he missed his mark. 'The sound

that came out from behind the front door was like dry concrete being blown into rubble by a powerful force—impossible to describe. That's when my legs finally moved.'"

"Robert backed away, rubbing his pained eyes. In his peripheral vision he says he saw a figure exit the house that chilled him to the bone. Whatever it was, was not gravity-bound, and was not like any animal he had ever seen. In fact, he wasn't sure if it was a solid being, an apparition, a gas, or a liquid, in true form. "It may have been all these...it may have been none of these."

"Robert was found half an hour later when another hunter discovered him lying in the clearing, disoriented. Eventually, he completely lost his eyesight, but still claims he can see the thing that blinded him hanging upside down from the porch of the Prestillion home.

"'It haunts me, really. I see it all the time in my mind.'"

John stopped scrolling. He felt the hair on the back of his neck stand, his flesh crawl. What *was* it that this reporter was describing?

John sat back, stretched, rubbed his eyes and yawned.

His eyes met with the side of the screen. The scroll bar was almost at the bottom of the page. There was not much more to study. So he leaned forward and read the last passage.

"Boy Dares His Own Sanity—The Chester Local—Saturday—2010

"Oscar Carrin was a respectable teenager with his head on straight, a 4.0 average, and a love for wrestling. He was planning to go to Harvard on a scholarship, but his dreams came to a crashing end when he was dared by a friend to venture into a house notorious for unexplained phenomena—the Prestillion House—one single structure surrounded by many locals who won't even mention it. Not a moment after stepping inside the place, Oscar ran out screaming, ranting

and raving incoherent ramblings neither of his friends on site could understand. His eyes, 13-year-old Rick Tollsen said, were wild, completely glazed over, and searching for something that wasn't there. 'I've never seen anybody look as afraid as he did then...not even in the movies. His other friend there at the time, Tom Peterson, claims Oscar's body was trembling so badly he thought he was going to hurt himself. 'He just thrashed his arms and legs. I don't know if he was trying to fight the air or get away from somebody.' Seconds later, the seizure broke, and Oscar fell limp to the ground. Neither one of his friends could tell if he was awake or asleep. 'His eyes were open, but I could tell he wasn't all there. I was just glad he had calmed down...but at the same time,' Peterson says, 'I would have rather had him shaking and screaming compared to what he started saying as he stared up at us, past us. Stuff like "don't look beyond the veil of," and "watch for the day when Sturpth opens its head in the sky of the burning star," and other things that didn't make any sense. The very last thing he said was "Rock a bye Rollings.'"

John shot back in his seat as if he'd been shocked by a taser. His hand began shaking, and his mouth fell open. "Rock a bye Rollings" was a phrase his mother used to say to him when she rocked him as a child. Oscar Carrin hadn't even born yet when she had stopped saying that.

He got up, looking down at the screen in horror.

He suddenly recalled her singing: "Rock a bye Rollings, my sweet boy John, a gift to the earth, with you there's no wrong, now go to sleep gently, and have a nice dream, when you wake in the morning we'll eat some ice cream." Not good enough for a Hallmark card, but it used to comfort him.

He hurried out of the library, unnerved.

Outside, the air had cooled a few degrees. Heavy gray

clouds blanketed the sky, masking the sun.

John jogged across the street, down the block, and down the alley, feeling eyes again watching him. Right now he didn't care to whom they belonged; he just wanted to get out of there, but once he reached his car, he fumbled the keys out of his left pocket. Someone, or something, was watching him.

He looked around and saw the Doberman from earlier sitting over by a row of dented garbage cans, panting.

"Are you all right?" As soon as he asked, the dog whimpered and walked his way.

"Are you okay?"

The dog's mouth curled up and back, revealing two slimy sets of canines. It was not a signal of an oncoming attack; it was more of a handshake. The dog was smiling. This made John smile in return. He knelt down and rubbed the animal's sides. "You need a name. Can't keep calling you—*you*. What are you, by the way?" He checked between its two rear legs. "You're a boy. Let's see. I can call you...how about Lucky?"

The dog barked, did a spin, and bombarded his face with a shower of kisses.

"Lucky, it is! Ease up, ease up."

Lucky complied.

"Well, Lucky," John said, standing back up and opening his car door, "thank you again for saving my butt, and maybe I'll see you around here again sometime."

As he went to sit down in the driver's seat, the dog whined and scratched at his leg, either wanting to go with him or wanting him to stay behind.

John shook his head. "You can't come with me. Dogs aren't allowed in my apartment. It's just the way it is. I have to go now."

Lucky whimpered some more.

Grabbing onto the door handle, he felt terrible having to

leave the poor stray behind, but he felt he had no other choice.

He pushed back the tears in his eyes, put the gear in drive and drove away, trying not to look back at the dog that had saved his life.

***

That night, John's head jerked from side to side on the coffee-stained pillow; his legs kicked and thrashed at the sheets and blanket. Moans escaped his throat. Dream images left as quickly as they came. John could not distinguish between any of them. His soul was flying through a milky mist filled with a cacophony of visions.

Then, a phantasm of Lucky flashed in his mind. The dog was sitting in a grassy field, looking off to the side, panting. He barked in slow motion, the sound deep and penetrating.

But, like a candle flame in the wind, it was gone, leaving behind nothing but a smoky impression in its wake.

John's head swung to one side, nearly colliding with the bedpost.

Then another image flooded his mind. A tall house that was at once old and new, derelict and immaculate. *The Mayberry House? No, the Prestillion House…isn't that what the newspapers called it?*

Instead of wood and stone, it was a shape-shifting illusion, a parody of the real thing, not bound by reality. As he stared at the mirage, wood, brick, and other forms of debris flew at him, pummeling his body. Then he was inside the house, in the foyer, lost, disoriented, bruised and bloody. The walls around and above, the floor below—all closing in on him. The room seemed to be shrinking, threatening to crush him. He could not draw even the slightest breath. He tried pushing the walls away. They continued inward, compressing his limbs, crushing them to his body. His elbow stabbed his liver, his legs snapped in half, and the bones of his skull cut through his brain. Blood poured from his nose, ears, and mouth.

The pain was unbearable.

More bones shattered, more cuts open, more blood spilled. *"Rock a bye Rollings...Rock a bye Rollings...Rock a bye Rollings,"* said a voice that most certainly was not human.

John jolted upright quickly, breathing hard and covered in sweat. The desolate, gut-wrenching feeling still lingered inside him.

CHAPTER THREE

John left his apartment moments after receiving a call from Charlie Steera. Today, the sheriff's voice sounded further unsettled, the content of his message bizarre and unnerving. Apparently during the night, one anxious officer had entered that house, wanting to see for himself just what was *really* happening in there. Moments passed without a scream or a whimper, and fortunately the man came back out alive, but was broken out in hives, drooling and screeching in an incoherent babble. He was taken to the ER for observation, where doctors found cancerous growths forming in various parts of his body, ruptured blood vessels in his brain, and a bleeding liver. John was still uncertain why Steera called him about this house, why he was the go-to guy for these events. What sort of expertise was the sheriff convinced John could offer? It didn't matter. He was involved now, and given his dream from the night before, it would be impossible for him to become uninvolved.

***

John threw open the door and stepped outside into another gloomy, dismal Friday afternoon. A small flock of geese flapped their way south underneath motionless, gray clouds. The ground was still wet from an early morning shower, and the sounds of water pouring into the sewers filled the air.

He removed the key ring from his pocket and went to his car. Sitting there beside a bright-red fire hydrant was the last thing he expected to see: Lucky.

The dog was simply watching him, panting, almost grinning. Its big black eyes sparkled brightly in contrast to this suppressive atmosphere. Drops of saliva flew from his mouth as he barked at John, requesting his attention.

How did this dog find me?

He unlocked his car, opened the door, and patted his leg. The dog ran across the road in an instant, kicking up black water from behind its weathered paws. He smiled as the dog jumped up on him and licked his face over and over.

"Lucky!" John laughed.

Its large, rough tongue jabbed at his cheek, nose, eyes, and forehead. Doggie drool dripped and oozed everywhere.

"Okay...that's enough."

Lucky stepped back on command. A car horn honked in the distance. A bellow of thunder tore through the sky, but Lucky didn't budge. He just attended to his new master.

John wiped away some slobber from his face and looked long and hard into the animal's eyes, astonished by how well it actually listened.

"You can understand me?"

The dog barked.

"You know what I'm caught up in, don't you?"

The dog barked again.

"You might be hurt by helping me."

The dog barked once more.

"It's your choice, my friend. Are you sure you want to come with me?"

The dog jumped into the car. John sat on the sidewalk a

moment, wondering if Lucky was maybe a guardian angel covered in short, black fur.

***

There was but one vehicle parked near the house on Mayberry Road: Steera's car, but the sheriff was nowhere in sight and the area seemed even more unnerving than any time before. Lucky sat in the passenger seat, seat-belt wrapped snugly across his chest, and panting heavily.

The dog whimpered when he turned his head to the right. John followed his gaze. Through the trees, over some branches, and past some bushes, a small portion of Prestillion House could be seen.

"Believe me, I know how you feel, Lucky."

Lucky looked back at John and tugged on the seat-belt with his slimy teeth. "Sorry about that. I know you didn't want to be buckled, but as if you couldn't tell, I'm a pretty bad driver."

The dog barked, then pawed at the door. John reached over and opened it for him.

"You need some fresh air? I know that as I—"

Lucky jumped out and darted into the forest before he could finish.

"Lucky! Wait!" John eagerly went to undo his own seat-belt. By the time he managed to push the switch, the dog was gone. Lucky had disappeared into the surrounding greenery, the loudness of his barks fading gradually.

John stepped out of his car and looked toward some swaying bushes. He listened for a moment, waiting— hoping—to hear something.

But no sound came.

"Lucky?!" He raised his voice.

John's eyes focused in on the leaves attached to the shrub's long, thin branches.

Then Lucky unleashed a torrent of growls. He had found something or somebody and, by his vicious vocals, wanted to tear it apart.

John took off into the woods, down the wild path, whose overgrown weeds were taller than just two days ago. His shoes left behind noticeable tread marks in the mud as he plodded through it. Lucky's rampaging bellows echoed all through the valley, drowning out every other natural noise.

Out of breath, John finally entered the clearing. "Lucky..." He looked up and saw before him, standing as tall as the tree, the house on Mayberry Road—the Prestillion House.

"Scared the shit out of me!" Sheriff Steera said. He was standing by a tree, his gun drawn.

"What were you going to do? Shoot him?"

"Hey, all I know is I was standing here, waiting on you, and this beast comes running toward me like a hungry black bear. I didn't shoot him, did I?"

John walked over to Steera, who holstered his Glock.

"Nobody's here but us?" John could not believe it.

"Safer that way."

"You sure about that?"

"John, I've had three adventurers go into that house 'cause they were overly curious, and look what happened to them. I can't have any more of my guys going near this place."

"Fair enough."

Steera looked from John to the house. "Are you going in?" he asked.

"Yeah. I have to."

Steera gave him a flashlight and a police radio. John approached the foreboding house with Lucky at his side. Steera watched intently from a distance.

John tip-toed up the three porch steps and turned on the flashlight. With one nervous, sloppy motion, Rollings turned his head and looked back at Steera, as if saying farewell before entering.

The door opened by itself with a groan. A musty, stale draft of cold air blew from the expanding crack, reminding him of the smell of his grandparents' attic. Finally, with all the courage he could muster, he and Lucky entered the house.

John's flashlight captured every particle of dust, dirt, and microbe floating in the air. Immediately to the left was a staircase enshrined in a case of cobwebs that covered much of the wood.

John directed the light to a room just past the stairs. The floorboards whined beneath his feet. Lucky followed closely behind, sniffling through the dust, unable to see much.

This room, though dulled with age, had a strangely homey feel to it. A glorious shaft of sunshine poured in through the arched window by the far wall, shined on an antique dresser, bounced off its cracked mirror, and radiated back out toward its original source. The source of light, which looked like the sun through the window, couldn't have been any such thing. The sun was obscured by cloud cover.

No. It can't be the real sun, John told himself as he stepped farther into the small, perfectly square room. Besides the window and crumbling dresser, a mattressless bed and nightstand were also inside. The metal springs barely attached to the rusted bed frame were sharp as razors, and the floor beneath them was scattered with feathers and clumps of a material John recognized quickly: asbestos. He covered his mouth and nose with his collar, just to be safe.

The frame of the bed, though chewed and destroyed, was too small to have held an adult. And when John's eyes shot to the far corner, through a piece of twisted bedframe and behind the stand, he realized that this was, or had been, a child's room because a one-eyed doll was staring straight at him. Its clothes were so dirty they were black, and its face was threaded thoroughly with sewing string.

The cold chills ran up John's back, came through his arm, and into his hand as he saw what he thought was the eye moving, following his shivering hands. The flashlight trembled. Lucky looked up at him, concerned.

"It's okay; it's just a doll," he told the dog, but what came to mind was the *Twilight Zone* episode titled "The Living Doll." *Are you going to kill me, doll? It's not going to hurt you,* came the answer.

The rubber in his legs made him so unsteady he almost crashed to the floor when Lucky ran out of the room and up the stairs, barking a most horrible sound.

John rushed to the stairs and aimed his flashlight up them. The dog was gone.

"Lucky? *Lucky!*"

A moment later, he could hear Lucky whimper, as if injured. Then the whimper died out immediately.

John hurried up the stairs, the flashlight in his hand bouncing around, its diffuse beam lighting up the banister with an eerie glow.

"Luuuucky!" John's scream sounded dull and harsh.

He ascended the remaining three steps in one stride. He turned to the left, and then turned to the right, searching for Lucky, but his dog was nowhere in sight.

And then another whimper....

"I'm coming, Lucky."

John continued forward, passing down a hall of closed doors.

He heard another whimper from a door that was ajar. In the glow of the flashlight, he could make out the dog's tail through the crack.

He opened the door quickly but gently. It creaked with the sound of an old car door. His eyes shot over to the window, then down at Lucky, who was staring at a figure bent down and turned away in the far corner. The being was entirely nude, its outward form flesh-like but scaly, its color one shade darker than pure white. It looked smaller than an adult, but larger than a child and shaking feverishly in a way that could have been either absolute fear or laughter.

Bones protruded from places where they shouldn't. Some of its limbs were bent at improbable angles. Its feet, for instance, were twisted backward and up, resting in a very painful-looking position where John could see its dark-blue toenails. Its quivering head didn't move like a human's, either, but in a much wider range of motion.

Was it *that*? A *creature*? Could it be? Some prehistoric mammal, or reptile, even, trapped in the Prestillion House and unable to leave?

John walked toward it, trying to make as little noise as possible, and slowly reached out for its shoulder. The floorboards wavered underneath its erratic trembling. He reached out and touched the being's cold, clammy flesh, producing a hissing cloud of steam.

It stopped shaking and twisted its head completely around without moving its torso, coming face to face with John.

They looked into each other's eyes without expression. "Hel—wh—just—I'm—an—" The words would simply not come out.

John concentrated, trying to articulate words that caught in his stomach.

Then Lucky growled.

The creature turned its head back an inch more and looked at the dog, an expression of stark horror manifesting on its face.

Suddenly, it stretched its mouth open so wide it could have swallowed a small football. John could see into the back of its throat. *What is it doing?* Lucky darted out of the room and down the stairs, whimpering and howling louder now than he'd done outside moments ago. The only window in the room shattered into pieces. John jolted backward, puzzled. He had no idea what was happening. Glass fell everywhere.

"It's okay. I'm not going to hurt you." He went to place a hand on its shoulder, but recoiled back into the corner. The small pieces of glass lying on the floor cracked and snapped apart.

"John, are you in there?" Steera's voice was tentative, full of concern.

John turned to the open door. No one was there. When John turned back to look at the being, it was gone.

The broken window was now unbroken, too. There were no shards of glass anywhere on the floor or sill. It was as if the house had repaired its own damage.

He left the house in a hurry and was greeted by Steera. "Jesus Christ, John, what the hell happened in there?"

John had no answer.

***

Lucky whimpered for many minutes; his ears continued to bleed. Lucky, John, and Charlie were sitting back in the parked car back on the gravel road outside the perimeter of the woods, trying to figure out what to do next. John looked withdrawn. His eyes glazed forward with no life in them at all.

"I think Lucky needs to see a vet." John didn't blink. The tone of his voice was lifeless.

"Now, I know this is hard for you, but what did you—"

"Charlie," John interrupted, "don't let anybody near this

freaking road again. I'm lucky—and Lucky is lucky—to have come out in one piece at all."

"Did you see something?"

"Whatever I saw—I *touched* it. I don't know why, but I did."

"Was it a ghost? A demon? What did it look like?"

"It—it was just like you and I. A living creature—flesh and blood. Anything else I could say would just be speculation. All I know is it seemed to be as scared of me and Lucky as we were of it."

Lucky cried. John petted him and smiled. "I know, boy. We're going to make you better soon. I promise."

CHAPTER FOUR

The following morning began with the sun climbing slowly over the hills of the Ohio Valley, its brilliance not impeded by a cloud in the sky, its warmth radiating the town of Bellsville. The rippling river reflected its gleam masterfully. Birds flew through the sky, their wings flapping in the cool air as they made their journey south before winter.

John was on his cell phone, still in bed, but dressed and ready to go. "So you'll meet me there? At Nineteenth-Street Park?"

The voice on the other end was old and scraggly. "Yes. How about at the bench in the open field? Y'know, where most people take their dogs? I'll be sitting by the big, twisted oak near the fountain."

"Sounds good. Give me about twenty minutes."

John snapped shut his cell phone and put it in his pocket. Lucky was sitting right in front of him, tail wagging, eyes innocent and curious.

Warf! Warf! Warf!

"Okay, boy, let me get the collar and leash. See if this thing even fits you."

John grabbed them off the nightstand. Both were pink, not a masculine color, but John had obtained them free from his cousin, Beth, after her Airedale was put down back in '98. He had stored them away in a drawer ever since, just in the likelihood that he ever did get a dog.

"Here. Let's wrap this on here." John knelt down and stretched the collar around Lucky's neck. It fit perfectly. He snapped it in place and hooked the leash through its loop.

"Okay, let's go."

Lucky barked and ran toward the door, yanking his master with him.

"Lucky!"

They entered into the cool, fall air, the furry leader bolting athletically down the five concrete steps, the lagging follower stumbling awkwardly to keep up. Both relished the pleasant atmosphere. John felt revived after a good night's sleep, during which he didn't dream about the house on Mayberry Road whatsoever.

All the better.

His head was clear, his stomach full, and his bladder empty.

Lucky slouched down on its front legs as he proceeded, sniffing the scent of another animal's recent trail. He deemed it necessary to stop and smell every fire hydrant, every STOP SIGN, every bush. John was patient with him. He didn't yank on the string once. He took his time, too, exploring the bleak little town that was dying instead of growing. The old Board of Education building, only nine years ago alive with teachers, coordinators, parents, and school board members, was now vacant, its structure overrun with stray weeds, its windows all cracked and broken.

The old dime store, once a popular business with kids and young adults, was now forgotten and out of business. Jobs were scarce here. Everybody was moving south. The winters were too cold, too long. The advent of cell phones had disintegrated physical human contact. People mostly stayed indoors and played games. When they did go out, they fed their paychecks to the poker tables or slot machines at Jack's Dollar's Casino. Just like any small community, Bellsville was suffering, taking its last breaths, fighting to stay alive.

***

Their walk took forty minutes, twenty more than John had expected. He tried phoning Father Henry three times during the way to inform him he was running a little late, but the battery in his cell phone had died.

Nothing like standing a priest up.

Still, he and Lucky were almost there, now crossing through a path into the local park, which, today, was crowded with joggers, bikers, and power-walkers, trying to get in that last bit of outdoor activity before winter set in.

Soon, he and Lucky crested a hill and walked past a sign, which read: *Mannor Animal Park. Please clean up after your pet. If you do not, you WILL be fined for littering. Thank You.*

They proceeded around a curve. Stretched before them now was a huge, wide-open field jammed with people playing with their pets. Lucky went ballistic when he saw the different breeds of dogs running after sticks, balls, and Frisbees. He tried to run toward them, barking, but barking was all that John allowed him to do.

"No, Lucky. No!" He had to hold the leash tightly.

Thirty yards straight ahead, a man in thick, black clothes was sitting on a bench, watching the animals play. The glasses sitting across his nose looked like they were going to fall down his nose. He was an older gentleman, probably in his sixties, thin, his hands covered in wrinkles. He wore a meek smile and a clerical collar on his clergy shirt. He seemed tense and uncomfortable.

"Father," John greeted, sitting down beside him.

Father Henry looked over. He pushed up his glasses.

"John Rollings. How are you doing? I haven't heard from you since you moved back here."

Lucky forged ahead, but couldn't get out of the restraint. Instead, he choked himself on the leash.

"Yeah, and I haven't been to church lately, either, Father. I apologize, really."

"It's okay." The priest glanced up at the sky. "It doesn't matter if you come to church or not. You're serving the Lord by caring for that dog. We all serve the Lord in our own way. That's what makes us unique."

John gave his own smile and petted Lucky. "How did you know?"

"He depends on you, John. Keep him safe, and he will do the same for you."

Changing the subject to what he really wanted to talk about, John said, "The sheriff—Steera—has me working with him on a case. I don't know why, but I guess you can consider me a volunteer detective…no, scratch that…a *paranormal investigator.* The house of Mayberry Road. That's the house where…where Sarah went before she died. And a teenager was killed there recently."

"I see." Henry coughed into a wrinkly fist.

"Father, whatever is in that house is beyond my ability to explain."

Father Henry suddenly looked disturbed. "John, stay away from that house. There is evil that makes even Satan shiver. You'll do best to avoid such things."

"I can't just leave the investigation behind. I *have* to dig deeper. I think I'm the only person who can enter that house without being killed or going insane. I don't know why, but it seems that whatever evil is going on there, I am the only person who can stop it."

Father Henry replied with sudden urgency: "Have Sheriff Steera tear that house down!"

CHAPTER FIVE

The following morning, John woke to the shrill of his ringing cell phone.

"Steera, is that you?"

"Yeah, it's me, John. I'm up here on Mayberry Road. Three local neighbors teamed up together and tried to burn the house down last night. Everything's FUBAR out here. Two just dropped dead, and one caught himself on fire at the last minute for—I don't know what reason. Four firemen went into the house to extinguish the flames. None have come out. The flames eventually went out by themselves. The structural damage—*Jesus*, there isn't any!" He paused for a moment, and then said somberly, "John, the man who caught himself on fire was Father Henry. Can you believe that?"

"Oh no."

"I might be called off this case soon. That means you, as well, but you have to keep on it. You're the only person who can enter that house without dying or going insane. The state commissioner is looking into this. I heard rumors that the FEDS might show up. So, if you're coming, you'd better leave now. And please leave your dog behind."

"I'll be there in five."

"All right. I'll wait for you at the road turn off. Like I

said, everything's fucked up."

John flipped his phone closed.

***

Two and a half minutes later, John stopped at the bent STOP-sign before Robin's Pike. Police sirens screeched in the distance. They sounded close. By the time John looked both ways and started up the hill, a slew of cop cars and one unmarked car sped down in the adjacent lane toward him, their lights flashing. They blew through the sign and proceeded toward the highway. John proceeded up Robin's Pike, around The Devil's Elbow (the sharpest turn in Bellsville), and across the dilapidated Red Winston Covered Bridge, whose recent paint job already looked centuries old. Many more vehicles passed him—not cop cars, fire trucks, or rescue trucks, but shiny black Crown Victorias with Government plates and tinted windows.

"You gotta be kidding me! FBI!" He watched them recede in his side-view mirror. This wasn't just a local matter anymore. The big fish had come to town.

He soon arrived at the entrance to Mayberry Road, where there was a nearly impossible to pass blockade. The entire road leading back to the woods was crammed with all kinds of personnel, even military. Two convoys were parked alongside the closest driveway. Men in camouflage stood around, directing traffic with glow sticks. Nobody was allowed to enter the restricted space. Surely not a civilian who couldn't even explain his involvement in this case.

A tall, young, muscular soldier standing in the middle of the road signaled him to turn back. He didn't look happy, either.

"John! John!" It was Sheriff Steera's voice. Steera was standing beside the passenger-side window.

John rolled it down. "Holy shit, Charlie, I thought there

would be a few out-of-town authorities here, but I never expected—the FBI? The fucking Marines?!"

"Yeah, tell me about it. They won't let any local authorities past security."

"Turn around and go back the way you came!" The solider walked forward, his eyes almost as fiery as the glow sticks in his hands.

"Look, John, I don't think we can stay here. How about I meet you back in town? We can talk about it there. You can explain to me the—" Before he could finish, the soldier in camouflage walked over to Steera and clutched him by his arm. "I need both of you to—"

Charlie yanked his arm away from the vise-like grip. "Don't you fucking touch me! I know my rights, asshole. I've been the sheriff in this county for longer than you've been alive. You're in my jurisdiction now, buddy. You don't know what you're dealing with in those woods."

"Listen, sir, I can have you arrested if you and your friend don't leave *now*."

John watched through his rear windshield as a flock of photographers took multiple pictures of the scene with their large cameras. *Click! Click! Click! Click! Click!* An enormous man with a rifle backed them away.

Steera continued, "Fine! Arrest me!"

"Sir, I'm going to ask you one last time. Leave the area. I'll even say 'pretty please.'" He moved closer, his face only an inch away from Steera's.

"All right, kid, the 'pretty please' got me," Steera said, holding up his hands and backing away, a sardonic grin on his face. "You got it. We're leaving."

The soldier watched him as he slipped into John's car. John immediately knew something was up.

"Don't tell me we're going to try blowing past security,"

John sighed.

Steera giggled, still looking at the asshole in camouflage. "If these fucking punks think they're going to kick me out of my jurisdiction, they got another thing coming. Meet me down at Pierce Run Road a few miles back."

"What's your plan? And is it going to get me shot or arrested?"

"Don't worry. If they just knew what you and I know, they'd realize they need our help." Steera stepped out of John's car, jogged to his car, and jumped in. John shifted his car into reverse and drove back down Robin's Pike. Steera soon did the same.

***

The branches of a dying maple tree scratched at each other in a chilly afternoon breeze. A few brown leaves coated some of the larger limbs. The steady pour of a nearby stream below filled the countryside with a bleak glimpse of life. The covered bridge over which it flowed groaned and creaked, its worn structure itching for someone to tear it down and put it out of its misery.

John and Steera met there less than five minutes later, right under the maple, between the faded covered bridge and the entrance to Pierce Run Road. "Okay, Charlie, I'm waiting." John stood beside the front right headlight of his car. Steera had just exited his own car, and was walking his way.

"Well, there *is* a way we can get around their barricade," Steera said.

John sighed. "You're talking serious trouble here. I don't fully know the laws, but I'm sure they would severely frown on that." He stopped, not knowing what else to say.

A harsh wind blew Charlie's hair, making him squint. "There is an old four-wheeler path that starts a couple miles up Pierce Run. It goes through the woods and all the way back to that house. We would just come out toward the east side, near the rear. They won't even know we're there, at least not until we let them know. I'll park a mile away in the woods just to make sure they don't hear the engine once we're close."

John seriously considered it. Venturing back into the unknown world of that house was something he wanted to avoid if he could. But what about Father Henry? John was responsible for his being out there, for him setting himself on fire.

John stared at the ground for many long seconds. His face was blank. After a moment, he looked up at Steera and shook his head. "God, Charlie, as much as I want to, I can't say no."

"Come on, John," Steera laughed. "Let's go."

***

John buckled in the passenger seat of the sheriff's car. "Hold on." Steera stepped on the gas pedal. His oversized hands yanked the wheel right. The car veered off the main road, passed between two trees displaying ripped and faded NO TRESPASSING signs, and ventured into a narrow wooded pathway.

"You sure you know what you're doing?" John held onto the door handle.

"Oh, sure."

"Okay, I trust you. I think."

Steera laughed and switched gears. The front of the car plowed through a group of small trees, snapping them apart like bones in a grinder. Brown leaves flew several feet into the air. John watched through his window as limbs and shrubs scraped against the glass, leaving behind dirt and scratches. Steera didn't seem to notice, or if he did, he didn't care. He simply drove, watching the road, or lack of one, ahead. John didn't believe Steera knew where the hell he was going, but he didn't want to say anything. Luckily, he had his recently-charged cell phone with him, so if they did happen to get lost or stuck, they could get help.

"Can you slow down just a little?"

"We're almost there! Have some faith, John. It's not every day you get an amusement park ride through the Bellsville woods."

"Yeah, but I didn't get my hand stamped to ride a rollercoaster, did I?"

Charlie's Nike-clad foot slammed on the brake.

"No. Don't even try it."

"This puppy can handle it. It's got four-wheel-drive. We'll be all right."

The puddle down the hill up ahead was as big as a small swimming pool. It was almost as wide as the length of John's Lincoln. A sloppy ring of mud surrounded the perimeter.

"Is there any other way around?"

"No."

"What if we get stuck?"

"Then we get stuck." Steera revved the engine. The car twitched.

The hill leading down to it was too steep, slick, and bumpy.

"You definitely better hold onto something." Charlie looked at John, who did just that. He clutched onto the sides of his seat, tense.

Steera looked right into the crater of brown water. His hand jerked the clutch. The cabin moved.

"Ready?" Steera smiled.

"I...guess."

"Trust me; it'll all be over within a minute. Afterwards, you're going to be glad we did it."

"I doubt that when your tires get stuck."

"You're just a half-empty glass of pessimism, ain't'cha?"

Charlie floored the gas. The car sped forward at top speed. Though stuck to his seat, John looked like he was about to fall out of it. Tires chiseled through mud. Chunks of it soared backward into the air, the tread mark of the tires imprinted on them. The steel beast proceeded down the sharp hill, slipping, skidding, finally regaining its hold on solid ground. John jostled from side to side, nearly bumping his head off the window and the ceiling. The puddle came closer. Small pebbles smacked off the hood. The front end careened into the puddle. Muddy water exploded into the air, splashing against the windshield, momentarily blocking both men's view.

A generous amount of smoke began to waver out from underneath the hood. The engine began to lose power.

"Come on. Come on." Steera pumped the gas. The wipers were going full blast.

"What's going on? We aren't stuck, are we?"

The front quarter of the car sat in the middle of the puddle, floating in spite of its weight. Seconds later, the submerged wheels found solid ground.

Charlie switched gears. His foot hit the pedal. Tires turned, but didn't grip. There was nothing for the rubber to grab onto, only slimy mud working as makeshift quicksand.

"Go, dammit!" Steera smacked the wheel. "Come on, baby." Steera gazed at the dashboard, his foot resting heavily on the gas. Water and mud gushed and sprayed from the exposed, spinning rear wheels, much of it drenching the trunk of a fat oak ten feet away. Bubbles gurgled to the surface of the puddle. The calm, mechanical hum of the motor filled the cabin.

Under the water, the front wheels managed to scrape

through a hefty layer of mud and find a large stone buried beneath. This gave them all the traction they needed to climb back out of the small pit.

"Alli-kazam!" Steera joked. Right when he said it, the cabin jolted, the monotonous hum quieted, and they were set free. The car climbed out of the puddle and up a small incline. They were back on flat land.

Steera shifted gears one last time and drove off into the woods.

From there on it took them only two minutes to get near the Prestillion House. Charlie parked behind a group of shrubs, hidden well out of sight from adventurous military personnel. They made their way across a small ravine flowing with clear stream water, and came to a large row of bushes near the east side of the house. Once there, they hunkered down, sheltered from view. They could see everything that was going on. The clearing was crowded with men dressed in jungle-camo and equipped with guns. Positioned straight ahead of them were three expressionless men in startling black suits. They looked like they belonged in a science fiction movie about extra-terrestrials. There must have been thirty people all together standing there like statues, watching as one tense, unlucky, sweaty cadet walked toward the front porch, pistol in hand, about to enter through the door.

John looked at Steera and whispered, "He'll die. We can't let him go in there!"

The sheriff pushed a bush aside. "Then go tell him. They'll arrest you before you even get to him. Let's wait and see what happens. Then we'll make our move. To tell you the truth, I'm anxious to see if that gun he's holding will protect him in any way."

John watched from twenty yards away as the soldier continued forward, the gun in his hand noticeably trembling.

He wiped away the sweat from his flushed face with his other hand. Steam poured rapidly from his opened mouth. Snot ran from his nose. He stepped up onto the porch slowly, and hesitantly reached for the knob.

His hand closed in on the knob. The index finger of his other hand was wrapped around the trigger of his Desert Eagle, prepared to squeeze lead into anything standing in his way. Sweat dripped off his chin, made contact with the door mat. Before the flesh of his hand even touched the rusty, worn brass, the door flew open, and something pulled him into the house. The kid didn't even get the chance to scream. The door slammed shut with a loud bang.

The men in black were no longer without expression. They looked dumfounded. All the other soldiers looked around at each other and shook their heads, all refusing to set foot near the building.

Everybody in the vicinity jumped when they heard the loud noise. Their eyes shot to the attic window as something crashed through it, out of it, and came spiraling down to the earth like a fallen coconut, trailing droplets of blood as it fell. It hit the ground, bounced off, rolled, and came to a stop by someone's military boot.

It was the soldier's head. His eyes were bleached white, his tongue dangling from his mouth, his expression bound forever in terror.

One soldier ran, another vomited, yet another fainted.

Steera laid his hand on John's shoulder. "All right, I think we can afford to reveal ourselves." As John lay on the ground behind a bush, Steera slowly and cautiously stood. "Excuse me. Everybody, listen."

The words were barely a whisper, but every gun in the clearing pointed his way. He raised his hands. Triggers were on the verge of being pulled.

"It's okay. I'm the Chester County sheriff, Charlie Steera."

"Who the hell gave you permission to be out here?" a man in black said, pulling a Glock from his pocket and coming forward.

Steera raised his arms higher. John lay still, not wanting to move.

"I don't exactly have permission, sir. But this whole thing began as my case. I've been on it for quite a while. I know how haunted this house is, and I may be of much assistance to you. I have with me the only person who has ever gone in that house and come out with his sanity intact."

The FBI agent continued toward him, gun aimed at Steera's face. The two other men in black pulled out their own guns.

John shifted as he felt cramps seizing his legs. He inadvertently moved a shrub. This startled the lead agent who rushed past Steera and aimed his Glock at John. This was the first time John had ever had a gun pointed in his face; he didn't much like it. It was like looking Death in the face.

"Whoa! Whoa!" John lifted his hands and rose to his feet.

"Who the hell are you? One of you tell me what's going on here, and *now.*"

"I'm John Rollings. I've been helping Steera on this case since a week ago. We came here because I figured out what is inside that house."

"What is your area of expertise?"

"Uh…I…I'm not sure. I mean, Steera just wanted my help." He didn't want to tell the agent that his claim to fame was hearing voices, or that he was psychic, for lack of a better term. "I'm the guy that can go into that house. I survived it. I think if you need someone to investigate it, I'm your man."

The Man in Black lowered his gun; as he did, the others

did too. Everyone breathed a sigh of relief. "You're a local, I presume?"

"Well, yeah. I think," John said hesitantly, "the only way to fix the problem is to go into the place. We have to know more about it. And I'm your man."

The agent pocketed his gun and looked disdainfully at Steera, then at John. His eyes narrowed. His mouth puckered at the corners. Then a smile appeared on the corners of his mouth. "You said you went in and came out once?" The agent seemed incredulous.

"Twice," Steera said before John could even open his mouth. His face was bright with a revelation. He'd just figured something out. He had an idea. "He went in twice. The first time, he almost died; the second, he came out relatively fine. It's like...he was *allowed* to go in. Remember the odor that seeped into your lungs the first night?"

John snapped his fingers, catching on quick. "Yeah!" He turned to the man in black, who was all ears. "It could have killed me...*if* it wanted. It wanted to send a message. To me. To all who wanted to learn of its secrets and expose them."

"Where are you guys going with this?" Another agent stepped forward.

"Well, if the master being of the house wants me to stay alive—" John began.

Steera finished his sentence, "—then why not bring someone in with you?" John looked at the lead agent. "Sir, if—"

He interrupted: "Vaul. Name's Vaul."

"If someone goes in there with me, they might be safer. Can't say for sure, but I would say it's worth a shot."

The man nodded without thinking. "Okay. Let's report back here tomorrow at six o' clock sharp, when we're fresh. Then we'll try again. I'll have some of my guys stay until morning to make sure no one trespasses." The men turned and walked away. John and Steera looked to each other, both gratified that they had gained approval with their on-going investigation of the house.

Neither man said much on the matter as they walked back to the mud-covered vehicle and headed back into town.

***

When he got to his apartment, he noticed the door was ajar; however, the lock and frame both looked in good condition. If someone entered the apartment, they didn't open the door by force. *Did I leave it open like this?*

He entered the apartment, peering cautiously about. He searched through all his belongings to make sure they were still there. The place looked no different than when he'd left. Lucky was fine. He was lying in the bathroom by the toilet, snoozing. John spent one whole hour looking for proof of an intruder, and finally found it when he entered his bedroom. Instead of anything missing, he seemed to have actually *gained* an item. An intricately designed, handcrafted dream catcher hung from the only window in his room.

A million questions boiled inside his far-stretching mind. Who had left it? How did they get in? Why did they leave it? What did they know about his dreams? Did they know something he didn't? Did this have anything to do with the case he was investigating? What were they trying to tell him?

A satisfactory answer evaded him. He hadn't a clue. He was too drained to really care at the moment. So instead, he got into bed and fell fast asleep.

***

Shrip. Shirp. Shirp.

The clipping sound of scissors struck his ears, loud and echoing. He could see a close-up of somebody's hair being trimmed with the gleaming metal blades, but could not make out the barber or the customer. In slow motion, thin, light strands of hair fell to the floor, where a small heap had already accumulated. A broom then entered the picture and brushed it all into a pan. Whoever swept it up, carted it off to—

Then John found himself surrounded by clouds, gliding through wind and soaring effortlessly into the light-blue sky, the sun gleaming against his smiling face. He did not glance back at the tragic world below as he distanced himself farther from its eternal chains. The warm fuzzy feeling in the pit of his stomach told him not to worry, that he was quite welcome where he was headed. In the immediate distance, he heard a voice he hadn't heard in almost ten long years.

"John. John." It was his mother's voice.

The clouds gave way, opened up, and he began to slow down rapidly. Thin, warm fog steamed off his heavenly figure. He was wearing a blinding, white robe.

"John!" His mother walked out of thin air and stepped onto the large cloud. She looked as he remembered her, but so much more vibrant and beautiful than in life, her face unmarked by a solitary wrinkle, her skin oozing pleasant pink light. Her joyful smile almost brought tears to his eyes. "Mom, is it really you?"

"John, I missed you."

"I missed you, too, Mom."

The robe she was wearing, unlike his, was fluttering in a warm breeze. Her hair was now the color of gold, her eyes the color of emerald.

"Is this Heaven?" He wanted to cry, but was unable to.

"You're in a place between Heaven and Hell." She smiled. "Walk with me."

They walked across an endless bubbly stretch of cloud. "Don't worry, son, you won't fall out of the sky." Then his mother paused in step as well as speech, and then spoke softly after a moment, "That's some investigation going on down there in your world. You and the house on Mayberry Road, the Prestillion House, as you call it. I've been tracking your progress. We all have. What you're up against is divinely monstrous, very powerful." Her voice was so quiet that John thought maybe what she was saying was forbidden. "This entity is real and powerful. Many I've talked to up here can't tell me much beyond a description of what it looks like. Twenty-two eyes, a profound knowledge of mysticism, and can reshape space. But, just like there are prohibited texts on Earth, which people aren't allowed to read, there are up here as well. I don't have the authority to look further into this mystical monster."

They began walking again side by side.

"John, I want you to remember that there are forces at work in the world above you, some below you. None of them have complete control of you. Some can hurt you. Some can help you. Some can save you. The ones with the bad intentions are the ones you have to keep an eye on. They're flawed like you. The thing in that house is, too."

"What do you mean?"

"Does Rock'a'by Rollings ring a bell?"

John swallowed hard.

"The entity discovered that *after* I sang it to you. It picked up on your trail. Yet, it still can't see as far as it wants to."

"What are you saying?"

"John, why do you think you went back there? To Bellsville?"

"I...don't know."

"Reasons for everything. You just have to find them."

"I don't know why you won't tell me. I mean, I need to

know. You keep hinting, but you don't give me anything concrete."

"The world is more fluid, John."

"What should I do then?"

She smiled. Her eyes lit up. Another warm breeze blew by, ruffling her robe again. "You know what you should be doing, John. You've always known. It's the reason why you wake up in the morning. It's the last thing you think about before you go to sleep. You're already doing what you're supposed to be doing, what God commands of you. Everybody has a purpose, even serial murderers. But yours is one of a kind. It's the universal connection of all living and non-living things." John didn't know what she was saying. "Do you remember that girl named Sarah?"

"I don't want to talk about that." He looked away.

"You're going to have to face it sooner or later."

"No!" He raised his voice. "It wasn't her time. She wasn't supposed to die. Not by suicide. If it weren't for me, she'd still be here!"

"Is that so? How can you be so sure?"

"Mom, I basically put that noose around her neck and pushed her off the chair. She died because I took her to that house!"

She shook her head. "It's not like that, and you know it."

"Then what!"

"You must go, John." She smiled at him as her pulsating form soared and disappeared.

***

Warf!

It was the sound of Lucky's bark.

John opened his eyes. He was laying on his stomach, his arm dangling over the edge of the bed, his face being attacked by Lucky's steady barrage of kisses. Doggie drool oozed off his chin.

"Lucky!"

The dog stepped back and barked again.

"What do you want? Outside?"

Lucky barked twice, his tail swinging from side to side.

John slowly and lazily climbed out of bed. His hair looked as if someone had taken a weed whacker to it. Bright sunshine beamed through the window, blinding his sensitive eyes. He could not open his lids more than halfway. Lucky, on the other hand, was full of energy and ready to start the day anew.

Warf! Warf! Warf! Warf!

"You better be quiet. Neighbors hear you and tell the landlord, and then you're right back out on the street."

Lucky sat down and whimpered. His owner leaned down and patted him on the head. "That's a good boy. Yeah."

In the dog's eyes, John saw the reflection of the dream catcher dangling in the window. However, this morning, there was something different about it.

John stood, turned, and stumbled over to it on wobbly legs. The threaded webs inside the capsule looked thicker than yesterday, and darker. Some were broken. A part of the surrounding cylinder appeared cracked. When he stepped right up to it to get a closer inspection, he was shocked to see what had actually happened. The webbed strings were covered in a thick, gooey slime, which felt like tar and smelled like burnt flesh. Tiny white crystals were scattered sporadically inside the gunk, obviously some sort of organic compound needing further investigation. On the innermost edges of the wooden ring were small marks or scratches, as if something had tried to force its way through.

But it was the heaviness of the dream catcher that really caught John's attention as he lifted it off the top of the window frame. Whereas it weighed a mere three ounces yesterday, it now weighed at least three pounds today. He was holding another world in his hand, a three-pound physical specimen of a horrible nightmare.

CHAPTER SIX

After John took Lucky for a walk and upon return, he got ready to head out to meet Steera.

During the drive to the house, John felt increasingly fatigued and nervous. Moments later, he braked at the bottom of Robin's Pike, roughly two miles from Mayberry Road.

The military apparently had the entire Pike blocked off. A guard didn't only request John's name; he requested to see his I.D., which he showed him.

"Okay, go on through."

Four other soldiers equipped with M-16s moved a barricade aside just far enough for his Lincoln to pass through. John drove up the winding curves of the Pike, passing by army truck after army truck, military officers surveying the land, and country homes, which all seemed vacant, their driveways void of any parked vehicles. Soon he approached the green metal sign that read: *Mayberry Road*. It was weathered, barely hanging onto the bent and beaten pole, a symbol now of great mystery and remembrance. His equally weathered car drove down the rough gravel terrain, toward many other parked military jeeps and trucks, and one vehicle John knew well—Steera's decorated car. John parked behind some unmarked crates stacked upon each other near the entrance to Runner's Stream.

Before he got out, he took a moment to gather himself, to put a leash on his tense nerves. His hands were visibly shaking on the wheel. His foot was trembling over the pedal. His breaths were fast and erratic. He felt as if he hadn't meditated for ten years.

Negative thoughts wanted to form in his mind, but then he remembered his mom from the dream and how beautiful she looked. How much hope she had.

Slowly, the anxiety cleared, withering away in the cool winter wind.

He was okay.

He got out of the car and headed into the woods, toward the others. The voices of Steera, one of the men in black, and others, invaded his ears almost instantly. Through some leaves and branches, he could see the group of men standing around in the clearing, talking. Steera glanced toward the path every now and then, waiting for his counterpart to arrive. John appeared a moment later.

"He's here," Steera told one of the MIB. The man turned and looked at him as he approached. Everyone else in the clearing glanced back, also.

"You're late!" The lead agent gave John a stern look. He pointed to his watch. "Six-oh-seven!"

"I'm sorry I'm late," John said with his head lowered, reluctantly joining the crowd. The three agents barely moved a muscle. Still, he could sense their extreme dissatisfaction.

"We're out on a limb for you, Mr. Rollings. If you want to help us, you must follow protocol. That means if we say six o' clock sharp, that means six o' clock sharp. Not six o' one or six o' seven. Do I make myself clear?"

John didn't really want to respond, but he eventually nodded.

"Good. Now here's how it's going to be. We're sending a group of you men in there with some high-tech machinery to figure out exactly what we're dealing with, down to the tiniest detail. The equipment will read such things as sounds undetectable to human ears, thermal radiation, hot or cold spots, unusual electronic signals, and foreign frequencies. In addition to these, you will be equipped with micro cameras, so that everything you see, we will see out here."

John glanced around at all the soldiers. They looked like scared children afraid to move. Some were trembling. Others kept looking around, paranoid. None of them wanted to go inside, not even John. The calmest-looking one was Steera.

"What about guns?" a soldier finally spoke up. "I ain't going in there without a weapon."

"Yes, in case of danger, you all will go inside with a firearm."

"No," John disagreed. It came out without warning. "No weapons whatsoever. Whatever lives in that place can see us. It can hear me talking now. If it can do that, it will know we're a threat when we walk in there with something possibly capable of destroying it. Guns may or may not work on that— thing. But if it sees beforehand what we're going to do, I believe it'll attack us fast, and probably kill us as quickly as it did your man yesterday." John could feel the presence of eyes upon them. He couldn't say for sure, but it certainly felt like they were being watched.

The soldiers shuddered. Vaul carefully thought over John's advice, and then looked into his eyes. John stared back. He knew the strange-looking government official was considering his suggestion, weighing it on his shoulders.

Finally, he spoke, "Okay, no guns. No weapons of any sort. Four of my guys and you, Rollings."

"Three guys and me," John said.

The first signs of life appeared on Vaul's face—disgust and contempt. "Excuse me? I know you're trying to help, but are you giving *me* an order?"

John looked at the sheriff, who shook his head, as if saying; *don't go there with this guy.*

"I'm not giving you an order, sir. I don't think it's wise to send an odd number of guys in there. I think we should group up in twos. Six may be pushing it. I don't want to be responsible for more possible deaths than need be. If four of us go in, we can split up in twos. I think we'll be safer that way."

Vaul put his fist up to his chin and paced, thinking about John's new request. One soldier, a seven-foot-tall black behemoth with a chipped front tooth, repeatedly coughed into his fist. He was taller and bulkier than the rest of his comrades, and appeared the most frightened.

"Okay." Vaul nodded. "Four men, but I pick who goes. Do not give me any more suggestions, John."

Vaul eyeballed the group of soldiers. Some men stood up straight, chests out, stomachs in, heads back, eyes front, like recruits in Boot Camp. They were all sweating, and it was not the least bit warm outside today.

"You." He pointed to one of the stiff-standing gentlemen, a short, bald, older solider. This man wiped the sweat off his forehead with the back of his hand and stepped up next to John and Charlie.

Vaul continued examining his choices.

"You." He pointed to a tall, lean man with piercing green eyes and a strong jaw line. "And you." He nodded at the short, muscular Hispanic fellow.

Vaul stopped pacing, thinking who to pick last.

"And...you." He lastly motioned to the gigantic black man, who vomited, drenching his right hand with orange fluid and cereal. Every one of the nearby soldiers jumped back, revolted. The shortest one among them covered his own mouth, holding back his own stomach juices.

"Sorry," the man said. The others backed farther away from him. "Just nerves, I guess."

"All right, men." Vaul did not sound enthusiastic. "You three, and you, John. Take ten minutes to gather yourselves and gear up. Report back here at six thirty." He looked directly at John. "Sharp!"

***

The twelve soldiers turned and walked back toward a group of crates where they prepared the electronic gadgets for field use while the unfortunate guinea pigs shook hands and exchanged names.

The black man approached John. "You said you been in there twice?"

"Yes. Name's John Rollings." He offered a hand.

"I'm Bud. Bud Carson. At least that's what it's gonna say in the obituary next week." His voice was sharply southern, and his handshake brutal. His breath reeked of bile. "Hopefully you'll be our battering ram, so to speak, into this hellhole." He laughed. John didn't join him.

Another man stepped forward. "Hi, I'm Jesus Garcia." The fit Hispanic man shook John's hand quickly and lightly. His palm felt like a wet sponge. "Do you think we stand a chance in there? I mean—"

"I can't give you any guarantees, Jesus, sorry. I wish I could. This is as unpredictable as it gets."

"My name's Bill Johnson," the next soldier said, nodding to John instead of shaking his hand. He didn't have so much as a single hair anywhere on his head, and was not even five feet tall. "War is unpredictable, sir. But God is on my side, so I will do my best."

"You don't have to call me 'sir.' And I hope we do have God on our side today," John said.

A few minutes later, as they were waiting to go in, Steera came up to John and asked, "You all right?"

"Going in there sucks everything out of me. My legs don't want to support my body, my mind does flips around my skull, and I can feel my blood flowing through my body like the damn Niagara. And yet, I have to do this."

"You *will* be all right."

John glanced up at the sky. "How can you be so sure?"

"I just know."

John looked at him, expressionless.

For the next five minutes, John and his acquaintants were fitted with enough electrical and mechanical equipment to build a small power-station. Soldiers crowded around the four investigators, planting various futuristic-looking devices in a plethora of places. Afterward, the four joined in the middle of the clearing, now fully equipped with head-mics, cameras, meters, detectors, and temperature-reading gauges.

"Whatever you see," Vaul said, looking from man to man, "you say on your mic. Don't try to be heroes, just do your research. We need to know what we're dealing with, not whether or not you can kill a monster. This is do or die time, gentlemen. If you see anything funny or are attacked, regroup immediately. God be with you."

The faces of all four men went pale with uncertainty and doubt. They stood in place, not wanting to budge. Their muscles failed to comply with their will.

John broke the silence: "Come on, guys, let's go."

He led them toward the house. The soldiers followed him up the porch steps, holding onto meters and junk they would have traded in for a good brick of C-4 in an instant. John slowly grabbed the doorknob, twisted and pulled. The mouth of the beast opened with a creak and gust of cool, dusty air. They all entered reluctantly, the ones in the rear more so than the ones in the front. From thirty feet away, the remaining soldiers and agents watched them disappear as the door closed behind them.

***

"Turn the sound on," Vaul barked at a young man with bad acne. He did as he was told. Voices entered everybody's ears. The agents crowded around the small televisions. The other soldiers huddled behind them, trying also to see what was going on. Nobody in the house was visibly moving. They all stood by the front door.

"Yes, I know. You two investigate the whole downstairs, basement and all," John told Bud and Jesus. "Bill and I will go upstairs."

The four split up into two teams.

On the monitors, the inside of the house looked unkempt. Dust and dirt fogged up most of the LCD screens, and the audio popped and cracked through the speakers.

"We—re get—a—lot of—act—with—the—" It was no doubt John's voice, but the signal was already breaking up.

Vaul ran a hand through his hair and sighed, frustrated. He gazed at the technician as if it were his fault. "Steve, you're *sure* this equipment is functioning properly? You've tested it before they went in there?"

"Yes, sir. Everything was in fine working order."

"What the fuck was that?!" One young soldier pointed at a monitor. Out of everybody standing around, he was the only one to have seen it. It came and went in a fleeting instant.

Vaul gripped him by the shoulders. "What did you see?" Everyone looked at the man, whose nose began to run with blood.

"I don't know what I saw. A face. A twisted face. I saw past its twenty-two eyes! I saw into its rabid soul...if that's what *it* was." The man's eyes were hazy, fuzzy, devoid of vitality. *"Ahhh!"* he cried and shoved his hands into his eyes. *"My eyes—they're bleeding!"* Vaul could see bleed streaming down the man's checks from underneath his hands.

"Holy Christ!" someone amidst the crowd gasped, horrified. Someone else backed away. More crackles of electrical noise popped through the speaker. One monitor turned to static. Steve said, "We got one out. Camera One is down."

The soldier with the bleeding eyes suddenly turned and ran off, out of the clearing and deeper into the woods.

"Hey! Come back here!" Vaul shouted after him.

No compliance. He looked at the other soldiers and ordered, "Go get him!" Two camo-clad men ran after him.

Vaul looked back at the monitor. Suddenly, the second camera fizzled out. "What's happening in there?"

"I don't know, sir." Steve shook his head. "It's as if the electrical signals connected to the motherboard are being manipulated."

"Manipulated by what?"

The man looked up at him but said nothing. He didn't have an answer. "It's very reliable equipment. My guess is whatever is in that house is affecting the feed."

"This is bad." Vaul glanced up at the house. As he did, he could have sworn he saw the porch roof curve downward in the center and curl up at the sides as if it were smiling at him.

CHAPTER SEVEN

Inside, John and Bill reached the top of the steps. A beeping sound reverberated through the hallway. Bill looked down at the thermonuclear detector. It was picking up a high reading of local radiation.

"Whoa, wait."

John stopped and looked back. "What is it?"

"This meter's going haywire on me. The radiation level is through the roof."

"Mine isn't beeping, Bill."

"Maybe yours isn't working."

"They're both working. Yours is being influenced."

Bill looked up at John, unnerved. "Influenced? You mean—?"

"Yes. By whatever possesses this place."

"What if mine is the one that's working and yours is the one being influenced?"

"If you want, you can turn off all your equipment."

"If the guy in charge out there sees you do that—"

"Don't worry, they won't. Those monitors outside aren't receiving any more signals."

"And how do you know that?"

"Just a guess, but I think I'm starting to understand a few

things about how this place works."

***

Out in the woods, a bush quivered as someone brushed hurriedly passed it. An army boot splashed into and out of a puddle of water as the soldier wearing it raced away.

"Hey! Wait!" one of the pursuing soldiers ordered. The man with the bleeding eyes kept going, smacking his face into some thick branches. Despite his obvious handicap, those pursuing him had a hard time keeping up. He was almost out of sight, running almost faster than humanly possible. They saw his trail of blood on the leaves, the ground, and the bushes by which he'd passed. Then the man vanished into thin air.

They stopped and looked around, searching for him.

"Where the hell did he go?" the leader of the two asked.

"He ran around that oak, and never came out."

They looked down the slope, past a tree, and at a stream. The current of water was strong, and a loose camouflage jacket soon floated along with it.

The two men slowly and cautiously hiked down the hill, each removing a pistol from his pocket, just to be safe. The only sound they heard was the steady flow of running water. The army jacket traveled about thirty more feet before snagging on a twig. The soldiers edged their way around the fat oak, tip-toed behind a bush, and came out on the other side.

Neither man could believe his eyes.

The man's back was turned to them, his body completely bereft of clothes. His army pants and underwear lay in a heap beside a rock. He was hunched over like Igor; his head tilted back, his eyes gazing up at the sky. He bowed a dozen times, as if worshipping the sun. Sounds came out of his mouth, but they didn't sound human.

"Harold?" One solider stepped forward.

He bowed one last time, then slowly turned his head to look at his two pursuers. His face was red, broken out in painful-looking sores and blisters that peeled and turned to ash right before their eyes. His eyes were solid yellow. The expression on his face was nonhuman, non-animal, and unearthly.

"Harold?" The other man stepped forward. "What the fuck happened to you—your face, your—" He pointed to his back. Orange hair poked through every pore violently and speedily. His spinal column quivered beneath his skin. The snapping of bones cracked through the air.

"Man, what's happening? What the fuck did you see on that monitor?"

"I saw the seven children of D'kourikai. What do you want from me, you little white dwarfs? What ugly, twisted beings you are." Its eyes shifted from yellow, to milky white, to black. More hair ripped through its tough skin, which began to sizzle and smoke the color red. The two men holding the guns began to drool on themselves. Blood began to run from their nostrils. Their hands trembled so harshly had they fired, they would have most definitely missed.

"You think you can end me with your lousy weapons? Only in this world, never in mine. You can't touch me in either with your hands—that's what you call them? Your verbal attempt at communication with these voice boxes is mediocre at best."

But the two humans could hardly communicate at all. They were in shock, too riveted by this otherworldly creature to utter even a groan. Both their index fingers had the trigger pulled back almost all the way, and neither was aware of it.

Harold's deformed back continued to grow with orange hair. The hair on its head curled and fell to the ground, where it evaporated in a boil. Its eyes shifted colors again, matching every hue in a Crayola box. Its lips bulged out, ripped unpleasantly apart, tearing and oozing a sticky green slime, through which brown-colored teeth emerged. Its hideous face ran with blood, *poured* with blood, and the pimples and diseased flesh grew and twisted in circles. The smile it gave the two soldiers made one of them piss his pants. Startled by the warmth in his groin, he finally pulled the trigger.

Before the bullet reached it, it disappeared.

***

Back in the clearing, Vaul pressured the technician to fix the electrical equipment from the current location. The monitors were still out, and only the sound of static was getting through the speakers. Seconds ago, Vaul had sent three more men into the woods to see what the gunfire was all about. He didn't feel in charge anymore. Everything was going awry. He did, however, feel the house still smiling at him.

"Come on, Steve. We have to get in there and see what they're doing. They could all be dead by now."

Steve pushed buttons, turned switches and smacked the machines, trying to force it to work.

"The problem is that the signal is dead, sir."

"And by your hitting this expensive equipment, you think you can revive it?" Vaul's face turned red. He rubbed the back of his neck.

Steve unplugged some wires, switched them, checked the power over to make sure it was on. His eyes stay glued to the blurry TVs. His right hand kept moving to the bulky headphones affixed to his head every time he thought he heard an interruption in the constant *shhhhhh.* Sweat poured down his face. He hated being under this much pressure. He could feel several steel-cold eyes watching his back, waiting very impatiently for him to fix something he couldn't.

"Anything?"

"No, sir, not—wait. *Wait.*"

He touched his headphones again. The static stopped. A faint, continuous buzz entered his ears, like the steady flat-line of a hospital monitor. Yet, he had never heard anything quite like it before.

"What do you hear? What is it?" Vaul was standing so close to Steve, it made him uncomfortable. The soldiers gathered around also, a swarm of camo-clad men anxious to hear the reply.

He listened closely. Intertwined with the whine, which began to slowly fade out, was an unusual sputter of broken syllables that had the elevated pitch of a screaming hyena, but was alien in structure.

When Steve looked up at Vaul, he saw his lips moving, his face flush. Vaul was obviously yelling, but he could *not* hear him at all. So he took off the headphones.

There was still no noise, no a sound whatsoever. Only a dull roar in his ears.

Freaked out, he jumped to his feet and ran out of the clearing, toward Mayberry Road, not once looking back. Everyone watched him go, mystified by the extreme terror engraved on his face as he retreated.

***

Bud and Jesus had thoroughly examined the child's bedroom and now moved on to the living room, which was oddly devoid of furniture. The dust on the floor was so thick it felt like they were walking on ice. The air was dense and musty. The walls were broken in many places, the slats behind the plaster visible almost everywhere. There were recesses in two of the walls, the first which led into a closet on the left, and the second which led to a pane-glass window on the right. The field and trees outside looked extremely dull and artificial through the glass.

"Nothing about this place is normal," Bud said as he did a slow pan of the room. "Jesus, can't you feel it?"

"It's pronounced 'Hay-soos.'"

"What?"

"Nevermind."

"What do you make of this place?"

"It's not going to be a house on MTV's cribs, that's for sure. I do feel some emotional vibe, though."

"Depression?"

"Exactly."

"Me too."

Jesus opened the closet door. Something jumped out at him. He leaped back. Bud reached for his gun, and aimed.

It was a human skeleton that shattered to pieces as Bud emptied his Glock into it.

"Jesus!" Jesus cried.

"Do you always shout your own name when someone shoots a gun?"

"It's 'Hay-soos,'" Jesus said, not amused."Fuckin' damn!"

"Scared the shit out of me, too," Bud said, looking at the shattered pieces of bone.

Jesus looked back at his partner and then down at his smoking gun. "What the fuck are you doing with that anyway, man? You're not supposed—"

"Never mind supposed. Self-protection, y'know?"

"Defending yourself against a skeleton? Yeah, I feel so much safer now. Thank you for rescuing me, oh knight in shining armor. Are you going to sweep me off my feet and kiss me? I just might turn into a beautiful princess."

"Fuck you. You were here yesterday. You saw what

happened to those other guys."

"But like that John guy said—"

"It's all bullshit," he spat. "He's full of shit. Don't be so gullible." Bud pocketed his gun.

"Then how do you explain—"

"Hey, all I know is reality is reality. I don't know what's going on, but it ain't because of no ghosts, I tell you that. Would you go into a war without weapons?"

"No."

"Then there you go. There are some evil dudes in here. Evil dudes armed with crazy-ass shit."

Jesus knelt down and examined the broken bits of bone. The marrow inside them gleamed like red diamonds, and had been crystallized by some type of sudden change in temperature. He grabbed one small fragment with his fingers, but immediately released it when a sharp pain shot up his hand.

Bud cringed. "What's wrong?"

"It's cold. Feels like dry ice."

"How long you suppose it's been here? The skeleton and all?"

Jesus stood back up and turned to Bud. "I can't tell you that."

"Say *what?*"

"It's like in my high school chemistry class, when the teacher soaked a tennis ball in a vat of liquid nitrogen and shattered it. Well, I think this might be the same."

"You *think* it *might*? That's not certain at all, now, is it? Huh?"

Jesus didn't respond.

"Come now, let's check the rest of this damn house," Bud said, aiming his radiation meter at the archway leading into a small kitchen.

Jesus thought about turning back, going upstairs and joining John and Bill. Their voices were barely audible anymore. Their footfalls were an echo in his ears.

"You coming or what, man?" Bud persisted.

But he decided not to break protocol. The house wasn't that big, anyway. After exploring three or four more rooms, he could see the light of day again. Then he wouldn't have to be around this jerk any longer.

Jesus followed Bud into the next room.

***

The hallway was nothing like John remembered. It was wider and longer than before, consisting of at least one-hundred doors on each side instead of twelve—doors that seemed to go on forever. Knobs glistened faintly, and dust particles swam through the air. The room where Lucky had found the hairless creature was now a void so black it made both men reluctant to proceed. They set down their encumbering equipment and looked at each other.

"Okay, Bill." John took a deep breath."This is crazy. There weren't nearly this many doors before, but I think if we stay close the whole time, never more than two doors apart, we can get through this alive. If you see anything funny at all, just yell. And don't stop talking to me, no matter what. If anything happens, run to get me, and if you can't, get out of this house. Do you understand?"

Bill nodded and looked down into the everlasting darkness, which actually seemed to be growing closer. He had never been this scared before, not only because he was unfamiliar with this territory, but because he pictured *something* in one or any of these rooms that was worse than death itself.

"Remember, don't break communication. That's the most important thing."

"I won't."

"I'll start in the first room on the right, and you on the first room on the left. Okay?"

Bill nodded. John gave him a smile that was no comfort at all. "Let's go."

They walked forward together, the old chewed floorboards beneath their feet sinking slightly under their combined body weight. In the far distance, past the utter blackness, there were strange sounds. Both men shined flashlights, but neither beam succeeded in capturing anything but brass, wood, and plaster. Their shadowy figures crept along toward the first two doors set right across the way from one another. John grabbed one knob, and Bill the other. They turned them simultaneously. Gusts of warm air shot out from the expanding cracks as each door creaked open and they stepped into their respective rooms. As soon as their bodies completely cleared the hallway, both doors slammed shut on their own with a loud bang.

CHAPTER EIGHT

Jesus Garcia's dimming flashlight lit up an old gas stove covered in some type of blue rust. It was shiny, discolored, and smelled like copper. Tiny pinpricks of silvery aluminum glistened in it like glitter. While Jesus examined it, Bud inspected the rest of the small kitchen, which was hardly bigger than a small bathroom. The rotten table was broken in half, the middles resting against each other on the diseased-looking floor. Cabinets were engulfed by mold and ivy. The brownish-orange sink was filled with dark, intricately-designed, spider-like webbing.

"Maybe this house isn't so bad after all." Bud licked his lips. "I mean, besides the skeleton in the closet, there really ain't nothin' here. Come on; let's go explore the back couple of rooms."

Bud left to do exactly that, and Jesus caught up with his counterpart in a narrow hallway sandwiched between the basement and back door.

"Well, if we do a job, then we better do it right," Jesus scolded him as they entered the pantry, a small corner room on the far northwest side of the house. Old, black clothes littered the floor. Broken pipes jutted from one wall. The backdoor was barely intact.

"You sayin' I don't know how to do my job, kid? I checked the kitchen just like you. I almost saved your ass back there in the living room. You owe me."

"For what? Putting me in danger?"

"Da' fuck you talking about?"

Jesus pointed to the gun in his pocket.

"Lighten up. It's for *protection.*"

"It's a *threat—*"

Bud interrupted him: "A threat to what? This house? Like that stupid psycho mumbo jumbo upstairs? *Ewwww, the house is alive. It's gonna kill us all.*" He waved his arms around mockingly. Then he was interrupted by a loud commotion from behind the battered basement door. "What the hell was that?"

"Maybe something fell. It could be nothing."

"That wasn't a fall," Bud said. "It sounded like a wild animal throwing around garbage cans." He took out his gun and aimed his flashlight down the dim, shadowy hallway. Jesus tried to aim his light, but it shut off and wouldn't come back on. So only one beam captured the discoloration of the old-looking door; only one beam lent them vision to the chipped brass knob shaped like a lion. They slowly approached it, their pupils dilating as they progressed further into the darkness. Faint rustling sounds seeped through the door, and large pounding thuds from below reverberated through the floorboards.

"You go first." Jesus motioned for Bud to proceed. "You've got the gun." Bud just looked at him with contempt.

Boom!

Boom!

Boom!

The door jostled with each rumble.

"How about you go," Bud said, more of a demand than a

question.

Jesus shook his head. "I ain't got the gun."

Bud handed it to him. But Jesus shook his head again. "Hell no. I'm not the one who didn't follow orders. I ain't the one acting like a horse's ass, either...*Bud.*"

Jesus placed his hand on the doorknob, turned it, and pushed the door open.

"What's that smell?" Bud said as air from the basement pummeled their faces.

Jesus thought about it for a minute. It was a smell that made him think about his local pizzeria as well as vampire legends. "I think it's garlic."

"Why the fuck does it smell like garlic down here?"

"How should I know? Wait."

"What?"

"The sounds...they stopped."

Before either man could blink, something large, green and *slimy* streaked across the beam of mag-light, knocked Bud off balance, and sent the basement door crashing into Jesus's face. It broke his nose and knocked out two of his teeth, causing him to tumble backwards; somehow he managed to regain his balance. Bud, on the other hand, fell forward, headfirst down the stairs, disappearing into the blackness.

"Jesus! It's got me! Something's down here! Heeeelp!"

***

"John! John! Hey!" Bill cried, pounding on the oak door with the bottom of his fist.

Across the hall, John did exactly the same thing, but neither man could hear the other, as they were both trapped into the rooms they had entered.

John raised his head when he saw a glimmer of reddish-brown light bouncing off the door he was facing. It was a dull, static glow. He turned around slowly. The room in which he found himself trapped was completely empty, without windows. The brilliant, wicked light that surrounded him was coming from no direct point, but seemed to come from every direction and out of the air, itself.

Across the hall, Bill had his own encounter with the unexplained. A greenish, yellow light lit him up from behind. This one, unlike the other, flickered like a candle flame. He turned, much more nervously than John had, and shined his flashlight around the room. It, too, was empty, devoid of furniture, and windowless. But then it *wasn't* empty. It was as if the fabric of reality ripped open, and he was looking into another world. He saw fields of oddly-shaped hay growing out of rippling waters; flying objects, or animals, soaring through the cloudless skies beyond the ten-foot ceiling; vibrating shapes of undisclosed matter moving horizontally through a distorted plane of existence. He saw things that could not be, but were in ways that currently are. He could see through everything. Then he heard a familiar voice call his name..."Bill!"

He dropped his flashlight and almost choked on his saliva. He had not heard that deep, grainy, old Texan voice since he was eleven going on twelve—the day his grandfather had died.

***

Jesus sat motionless on the basement steps, gazing into the void, wondering just *what* had hold of Bud. He could see nothing whatsoever, but could hear the thrashing sound of Bud's body being thrown around recklessly, and the wet, *slithery* sounds of some large creature shifting about. He had no idea what to do. He had not been trained to deal with any situation remotely like this.

Below, a tentacle wrapped itself around Bud's leg and

slammed him into the walls, the ceiling, and the floor, breaking his arms and legs, as well as inflicting other serious injuries. His head was bleeding profusely, and his body was covered in cuts and contusions.

He could barely speak, but he somehow managed to scream: "Get my fucking gun!"

Jesus did nothing, did not move a muscle. He saw the gun on the second step. He was paralyzed with fear as he listened to Bud get the life bashed out of him. The noisy movement of the large beast grew louder. Deafening and violent.

"Get me—"

Bud's body slammed against a wall so hard the foundation cracked. Blood oozed from his eyes, ears, nose, and mouth. His mind spun, and without warning, he found himself lying in pain on the floor, but alone. Whatever creature had had him was now gone. A flashlight was now lying four feet away from him. He struggled through his pain to grab it. After several agonizing moments, he reached it and flicked on its switch, its beam illuminating a fruit cellar door behind the staircase.

One arm was bent at an awkward angle, and his ribs felt as if they were shattered.

From near the basement door, Jesus could see the light and Bud's bloodied, mangled body.

"I'm fucking dying here! Where the hell are you? Somebody! Anybody! Chriiiist!!" Bud screamed.

Jesus was still, unable to move, afraid that whatever was down there was going to get him next. He was ready to bolt for the front door.

"You pussy motherfucker! I swear to God, when I get out of this God-forsaken house, I'm going to beat the shit out of you. Jesus, help me! Do something!"

He still did nothing.

"SOMEBODY!" Bud screamed. Then he started coughing uncontrollably as he started choking on his blood. When he finally managed to get his coughing under control, he moved his head around to see if the light illuminated a possible means of escape. There were rows upon rows of metal shelves cluttered with strange and ancient machinery; walls plastered with dusty, intricate blueprints of some sort of exotic invention; the floors covered in rust, broken rubble, and garbage. It looked like some kind of make-shift laboratory.

What the fuck is this place?

The light lit up a work table, a sensory-deprivation tank, and a small silvery crystal pyramid, which appeared to be suspended in the air with no visible string and no base rested beneath it.

He finally saw the basement door that led to the backyard. Only a mere twenty yard crawl away. If he could only manage it.

Slowly, but determinedly, he wormed his way toward it, crawling across the cold dirty cement floor. Pain throbbed through his every muscle, every bone, as he propelled himself forward, yearning for freedom. He only wished he had his gun.

CHAPTER NINE

"I know you're here," John said, examining the room for a presence. The omnipresent light shifted to a color he'd never seen before, and a faint breeze from no known source ruffled his clothes, his hair, and blew *through* his body as if he, himself, were a ghost. The air was neither hot nor cold, but of some unidentifiable temperature he felt only in his bones.

Before John's eyes, an entity formed from a barely-visible, wavering white apparition to a more profound, transparent, bubbling mass, and then to a red, bulky, shapeless blob-like figure with no features or limbs. It took time for it to grow, to solidify into physical matter. The unpleasant sound it made as it passed through dimensions wreaked havoc on his ears. It was not slipping through worlds; it was *forcing* its way through them.

"Roollllliiinnnngggs," it whispered his name. Its voice was black and powerful; its horrible, multi-jointed limbs broke through its sharply-textured flesh; its head tore through the bottom of its squirming body; its tail popped up from the top of its behind. The creature was somehow upside-down and right-side up all at the same time. It was hanging from the ceiling, unbound by gravity, unbound by many human

limitations. Foam seeped from its lower—maybe upper—torso, and fell to the floor almost in slow motion. Twenty-two small slits spread apart in numerous places from which black eyes emerged. John wanted to run, but all he could do was stare at it and scream.

***

"Grandpop?" Bill searched carefully through the thickening mist with his eyes. He could see very little, and the batteries in his flashlight were dying as well. He waited—and hoped—the voice was coming from Jack Johnson, the man he hadn't seen for over a decade.

Slowly, the sound of wind filled the room, brushing the mist away and bringing with it a yellow glow of heavenly light. Enshrouded in it was a tall, silhouette of a figure resembling Bill's grandfather.

"Grandpop? Is that you? That can't be you."

"—et out!" the figure interrupted.

Bill took two steps forward. "But, Grandpop, how can this—"

"Ge-t-now!" The voice interrupted him once more, and this time he heard the words as plain as day.

"Get out of here now! Hurry! Before—"

And then the mist, the light, the figure, and the voice were simply gone.

Dust fell from the ceiling. The floorboards quivered beneath his feet. The walls on either side of him slowly began moving toward each other. They approached the soldier an inch a second, two bone-crushing slabs guaranteed to turn anything into a pancake.

Bill went straight for the door, pounding on it, yelling for help, twisting the knob. At one point he pulled on the knob so forcibly that it came off in his hands. The walls closed in on him, the room drastically shrinking from twenty-by-twenty, to fifteen-by-fifteen, to ten-by-ten. Panicked and terrified, Bill rammed the door as hard as he could, hoping a hinge would bust or the lock would break.

***

"So, at last we meet, Jonathan. Are you afraid? You quiver inside your body. I feel it. It gives me fuel."

"What are you?"

"Simple question...and you have so many you want to ask—*need* to ask. You're a slightly intelligent life-form, very curious, yet very stupid." The beast quivered as it laughed. Its quiet chuckle somehow reminded John think of war, death, and suffering.

"Stupid how?"

"There are two questions from the human. Ah, impatient creatures you are. You give me little time to answer the first. We are a life-form, like yourself. We exist in another plane of existence, a much higher plane. To us, you are but worthless ants." The thing laughed again. Foam dripped onto the floorboards above its hideous head. John hated the grin that appeared on its face.

"You've come through into my universe and—and *live* in this house?"

"Yessss." It sounded like a slithering reptile just then. "I am called D'kourikai. We are the perfect beings designed by Cthulhu, the highest of all the gods."

John recognized that name. He'd heard it somewhere before.

"Many parts of him exist in many different places in many different realms. He is unbound by time and space. One of your brothers has written about him, barely a century ago. A writer who encountered him in one realm or another."

"Lovecraft," John whispered, suddenly remembering where he'd heard the name. Then, "What do you want from me?" It was more of a hiccup than a question, as it came out almost involuntarily.

Its eyes changed color. "Now *that's* an intelligent question!" It laughed again, its whole body quivering violently.

"Everyone else who has entered this house has died or gone insane, but you have allowed me to survive. What is it about me?"

The being stared at him with a look of fascination. "Do you know why that sheriff drags you along? You can bet it's not for your personality or charm."

"Then why?"

"The same reason we haven't killed you yet."

"What is so important about me?" John had to know.

"You will know soon."

"I demand you tell me now."

It raised its clawed hand and brought it down in a swiping motion. Even though John was more than nine feet away, his shirt ripped open, and one long scratch appeared on his chest. "You demand nothing of me. Understand? This is *my* domain."

The entity suddenly vanished, followed by the appearance of someone else. It was Sarah Pouster, the girl John had drastically failed. She was standing on a wooden chair, dressed in the same clothes she'd died in, with one end of a rope tied around her neck and the other end tied to the ceiling. She was not transparent, appearing fully real. John could even smell her subtle perfume. Was it real? Was *she* real?

John knew in the back of his mind that it was a mirage, but that didn't stop him from running toward her as she leaped off the chair. He dove to catch her before the noose pulled taut, his hands outstretched, his knees scraping against the hard floor. He caught nothing. The chair, the rope, and the dead girl vanished. Gone like D'kourikai, whose vibrating laugh resounded in John's poor ears.

I failed her.

Then he heard Bill's bloodcurdling screech from the next room across the hall, breaking him from his thoughts of failure and regret.

CHAPTER TEN

Down in the basement, something wrapped around Bud's leg so tightly his leg snapped in half. The solitary *crunch* was as loud as it was painful. He screamed as the thing yanked him away from the door, his only escape.

The long, leafy limb wavered around relentlessly, swinging his now limp and lifeless body around like a child's toy. Blood flew everywhere, spraying, gushing, splattering. A torn human brain fell onto a shelf beside the door. An eyeball landed beside a small bucket near a drain. Strangely, one shredded leg fell upright on the floor, the knee bone sticking up through lacerated tendons.

***

The basement soon went quiet but for the sound of a few broken hanging lights swaying back and forth. Jesus just watched and waited. His eyes did not blink once. He liked the silence even less than the noise. He gazed into the void, wondering if Bud was going to reach out for help...or if the monster was going to yank him away from life and from reality. Still, nothing happened.

He stood paralyzed at the head of the stairs, having momentarily forgotten how to move, how to breathe.

***

Upstairs, John found the door to the room he was in open, so he bolted out of it, going to the closed door across the hall, behind which Bill was screaming.

"Bill?" John raised his voice.

No response.

"Bill! Can you hear me? Open the door!" He pounded on the solid oak with the bottom of his fist.

"Joooohn! Get me the fuck outta here right now. Help me! The walls are—"

He grabbed the door knob and pulled it completely off. "Can you open the door on your side, Bill? The knob's broken."

"—crushing me! Get me out of here! The fucking doorknob is broke!" Three sweaty, jittery fingers poked out through the knob hole, reaching for help. *"Break the door down!"* Bill screamed. John knelt down and looked through the little round hole. He didn't know what he expected to find, but he didn't expect what he actually found.

The walls were coming together like an accordion, not seven feet apart now. Bill was standing in the middle. He didn't have more than a minute before his body would be crushed beyond recognition.

John carefully and quickly examined the door frame. The door opened from the outside in.

"Bill, stand back just a little! I'm going to kick it in."

"Geeeet meeeee ooooout!"

John took a step back and lunged forward, striking the door full-force with the heel of his foot. The surface felt more like solid steel than wood, but he ignored the pain and kicked it until he thought he had surely broken his foot—and then kicked some more. It didn't give at all. No cracks...not even a smudge. Bill's intense pleas grew ever more intense and desperate. He was screaming for his life.

Bill was hyperventilating, trembling, crying. *What is going on in there?* His question was answered—at least partially—by the sounds of contracting wood.

Finally, Bill's cries for help ceased, and with that, a door knob in perfect working order appeared on the door.

"Bill?" John asked tentatively as he wrapped his fingers around the new knob. "Bill, I'm coming."

Silence.

He turned the knob and pushed the door open. It opened easily. On the floor, in the middle of the room, a twisted, lifeless, broken and bloody body of Bill Johnson lay in a crumpled heap.

***

Whatever had killed Bud now wanted to kill Jesus. As the *thing* reached for him, his paralysis broke, and he ran out of the pantry and into the kitchen, where he stopped when he saw the entire wood floor crawling with a blanket of bizarre, glowing insects. They smelled like sulfur and sounded like crickets. Their ribbed, transparent bodies didn't just pulsate; they changed from one color to another in opposing colors on a color wheel. The floor resembled a large blazing puddle of lava one minute, then a green, slimy plutonium-like agent the next.

Jesus did not plan on sticking around, even if it meant wading through this sea of otherworldly insects. He crunched his way toward the open entryway to the living room, not looking back when three huge, plant-like tentacles shoved open the basement door. Their suckers—which looked like tulips working also as *heat sensors*—wavered up and down and from side to side, searching, finding, and then zooming aside when they detected Jesus.

He ran into the living room.

A window big enough for him to crawl through was

within reach, but he wasn't getting there.

He was *stuck*. The bottoms of his military boots were sticky with insect guts, which seemed to be acting like some sort of very powerful glue.

Then the smell of something burning found its way up his nose and burned his lungs. He doubled over almost immediately as what felt like fire burst forth from his throat. His boots were melting. The insect remains were not only incredibly sticky, but seemed to be incredibly hot.

Jesus cursed and wiggled, lost his balance and almost fell twice, trying to yank his feet out of the tight black boots which were disintegrating under him. The fumes continued to burn his nose, throat, and lungs, but he thought he could manage through the pain as his body became acclimated to the vapor and as long as his feet themselves didn't start disintegrating.

He ducked down, grabbed his boot laces, and untied them as quickly as he could with trembling fingers. He could feel the heat of the acid brushing against the heels of his feet, could smell the smoldering of leather melting to the hardwood floor. His throat burned, and he was suddenly seized with a fit of coughing. He managed to yank his foot out of one boot just as a white flame engulfed it. His hands then shot to the other one. Face drenched in sweat, he tugged the string, loosened them, and pulled. A white flame shot out of the boot, burning his sock and blackening his foot, but leaving him fairly unfazed. He was now free, but he was light-headed.

The clatter coming from the kitchen, which he had all but ignored while dealing with his boots, grew louder. He ran toward the window and flung it open when he reached it a second later, his eyes wide and excited. But the life drained from his face when he saw that through the opening there was only a black freezing void leading to nowhere. Through the closed, upper portion of the window, however, he saw treetops and sunshine, a distant rainbow and soaring pigeons.

What the fuck?

He could feel something behind him. He did not want to turn around, but he did, anyway, drawing in one last breath.

It was some sort of plantlike creature, wet, slimy, shiny, its tentacle-like tendrils constructed from millions of smaller twigs covered with layers of foliage. He wasn't viewing the thing as a whole; the rest of its body was still residing either out in the pantry or in the basement. Only its three long, pliable, porous limbs were stretched around the corner of the kitchen doorway. There was no telling just how big it really was, and Jesus didn't intend to find out. Its petal-like suckers vibrated, making a low rumbling sound as the hundreds of them sensed the intense heat emanating from Jesus's body. He was just as strange and alien to it as it was to him.

He backed up so far against the window that he thought he was going to fall through it. Sweat dripped off his chin. The tips of the winding tentacles grew close to his face. Garlic-smelling-slime oozed onto the floor in thick, gooey strings. He just hoped if it was going to kill him, it would do it quickly.

"Please," he said, his bottom lip quivering. As soon as he said it, the tip of the closest tentacle split in half, then into four, like a blooming flower opening up to reveal four rows of hollow, dark-brown, razor sharp teeth.

Jesus wet his pants; he could feel it run down his legs and into his sock. Tears flowed down his face along with the sweat. He clenched his teeth as those before him readied themselves to plunge into his skull. He held onto life for one last moment. And then, just as he thought he had died, been killed instantly, the horrific mouth screeched in agony.

Jesus turned forward and opened his eyes, amazed to be alive. Hundreds—maybe thousands—of insects were crawling and jumping onto the tentacles, feasting and gnawing on its coat like termites on wood. Their tiny fangs drew green blood from its appendages. He slowly backed away along the wall, retreating from the mayhem.

The tentacles spurted blood and wavered through the air like broken vacuum hoses, trying in vain to shake off the bugs. Some of the nimble insects actually began burrowing holes through the massive being. Tentacles flew through the air, crashing into walls and breaking banister railings with tremendous force. The percussive force of the exploding banister threw Jesus to the floor, where those nasty little insects scurried across his body, biting him all over his back, legs, and arms. The pain was immediate and excruciating, burying itself below the wounds, as if some sort of venom were injected deep into his tissue.

The green monster groaned again, its teeth clamping together. Quickly, before it sustained any more injury, or even death, it looped around the doorway and headed back down into the basement.

The insects continued to bury themselves deep into Jesus's flesh. Surprisingly, the pain was gone, but as he began to smell the stench of cooking flesh, he knew the lack of pain was a sign of fried nerve endings rather than a signal he was out of the woods.

White flames engulfed his body, leaving behind nothing but ash.

***

Nearly half an hour later, a traumatized John Rollings walked out the front door. Everyone was surprised there were any survivors at all.

"Oh my God..." Steera gasped.

"He's alive..." Vaul grunted.

John nodded to the sheriff and then to Vaul. "This is why you guys need me."

TROY McCOMBS

CHAPTER ELEVEN

"You sure you will be okay, John?" Steera pulled up to the curb beside the United Apartment building.

John gazed ahead through the windshield, mouth ajar. "Charlie, I saw something today that is going to haunt me 'til the day I die."

"You know, why don't you take some time off? Take a day or two. Hell, even a week if you need it."

"There's no day off for me. He's watching me now. This house—or whatever's in it—is connected to me somehow. I think you know it. That's why it lets me live, while it kills everyone else." He paused for a moment, as if mulling over what he had just said. "You know, I'll see you later."

He got out of the vehicle and shut the door. Steera rolled down the window and called after him, "John!"

He turned.

"Take it easy."

John nodded without looking back.

***

John stumbled half-asleep through the dimly-lit hallways of the apartment building. The doorways on either side reminded him of those in the upstairs of the house on Mayberry Road. The distasteful lighting made the place look more inhabited than occupied. As he neared his apartment, he began to wonder if he was back *there* again...trapped, immobile, confined. Soon, however, a sweet, pleasant odor overwhelmed his senses. It was the scent of a burning incense stick. It was not just coming from a nearby room; it was coming from *his room.*

John immediately thought the worst, and even thought of going back the way he had come. Had *it* followed him here? Could *it* transport itself through time and space?

He tip-toed to his bedroom, took a deep breath, closed his eyes, and readied himself to confront the enemy. Swirls of smoke poured out into the hallway.

With a quick jump and a shout, he burst into his room. The person standing on a small folding chair by the window fell to the floor with a shout of her own.

The girl looked up at him, a startled look on her dark face. "Please." Her voice was uneven, but kind. She sounded, above all, embarrassed. "This isn't what you think."

"It looks like you broke into my room, Miss. I could call the cops right now—" He noticed the brand new dream catcher hanging from his only window.

"Please, there's no need to call anybody. Just give me a few minutes to explain, and I'll leave. That's all I ask. I assure you, my intentions are good."

John closed the door behind him, walked over to the girl, and offered her a hand and helped her to her feet.

"My name's John—"

"Yeah, I know who you are," she interrupted. "My name's Jennifer Stockwell. I live right down the hall from you."

John let out a deep breath. "Now, would you mind telling me how you know me and what the hell you're doing in my apartment?"

***

The two sat across from each other, John on the bed and Jennifer on the folding chair.

She drew a breath. "I have been dreaming about you for the past two months, your place in the world, and I do not know why. At first I thought it was just random reoccurring dreams of you, some guy I saw around these halls, but when I started seeing visions of my granddaddy standing at the foot of my bed, I no longer knew if I was awake or dreaming. He said you would need my help with the upcoming battle of 'adjacent dimensions.' He showed me things in your past that you regret, and small glimpses of the future—basically no more than snapshots of things to come. Still, I remained unconvinced, thinking I was simply crazy, but then my vision came true." She produced a newspaper clipping and handed it to John. He looked down at it.

It was a photo of Evan White, the same boy who had died in that house.

"I read this article in a dream *before* this was ever printed. I saw what he had seen in that house, and I saw what you've seen in your dreams. I was with you when you were flying to the house in the woods. It's evil."

John didn't want to believe her, but he did. Something about her looked honest, like she wasn't capable of making this up.

"The dream catcher?" John motioned to it.

She smiled and blushed. "That's such an old, simple custom of my ancestors. It's a neat principle, really. As you sleep, your inner-self absorbs parts of the outside world. The webs of the dream catcher consume all the good energy that enters into your dreams, and all negative energy goes through into the hole, reabsorbing itself to the outside world."

"It's weird you say that, 'cause when I woke up, the webs

were covered in some kind of...waste."

"We're not dealing with negative energy, but an unknown one. There's no telling what can happen."

"You took it down, right?" John asked. "The dream catcher from when you broke in—came in here?"

She shook her head. "No. I assumed you did."

John stood, troubled. He looked around the room carefully.

"Is something wrong?" Jennifer panned around the room, herself.

"Yes. If I didn't take it down, and you didn't, *who* did?" John went to the window and looked out to see if it had fallen, but it was nowhere to be found. "Did you get in here with a key?"

"Yes," Jennifer nodded, embarrassed again. "My brother's a locksmith. He was able to carve a key directly from the lock."

John hurried to the door, knelt down, and examined the lock. There was a large crack in the door frame, expertly glued together. "Hmmm, well the first time you came in here, I noticed the door open, but no sign of forced entry."

"Sorry about that. I thought I shut it."

"Doesn't matter. But now it looks like someone broke the door frame and then repaired it. I assume you're going to tell me that wasn't you."

"It wasn't. I have a key." As if to prove it, she reached into her pocket and pulled out a silver key. "See?"

"Someone else must have come in here, taken the dream catcher, and tried to erase the evidence they were here."

"I really am sorry for breaking in here, John."

It was water under the bridge at this point, and he told her so.

"Listen to me, Jennifer; did you see anybody in these

halls today, anybody at all that you haven't seen before? Did you—"

"No. I wasn't here most of the day."

"Listen to me. I don't want you to help me. It's far too dangerous. The things inside that house…they would either put you in a strait-jacket or a coffin."

She shook her head. "It's supposed to be this way! You need my help!"

"Miss, you have no idea what you're getting yourself into. Somebody in town, perhaps in this very building, may be helping the—"

"—the twenty-two-eyed entity!" she finished his sentence, her eyes twinkling. "I'm not asking you to let me help you; I'm telling you that you need my help, and I'm going to give it. You can't force me away."

He closed his mouth and raised his eyebrows.

"How does the entity see you?" Jennifer raised her own eyebrows. "How does it track you, watch you, observe you day by day?"

"I don't really know."

"I can't see into its world, but I can see into yours. Every vibe I've been picking up tells me it has a mark on you. It can keep track of you because it has something that belongs to you."

"It saw what my mother said to me when she rocked me as a baby—"

"It could see that because it's linked to you. It somehow has a *direct connection* to you. But it can't see everything about you. It doesn't have dibs on you twenty-four seven. The dream catcher proved it! It can see what happened to you long ago because that memory of yours is something that remains dear to you. I don't think it can see things you've forgotten or don't care about."

John stared her down and shook his head. "How could you know this? Seriously."

She smiled. "I wish I knew. I do believe that it is most afraid of what it isn't able to see in you. That's the downfall of every enemy. I think it's sending you the dreams to purposely shield your eyes from the truth." Jennifer looked past him, off into space. "I've had a reoccurring dream of somebody cutting your hair as a child. Seems so unimportant, and yet I feel there's vital importance in finding out what it means. There's a big answer there. The truth is in the details, John."

He, for a moment, almost felt outshined by this young woman. She knew as much as, if not more than, he did, without having entered the Prestillion House. And here he thought he was the most elite psychic in Chester County. Was she right? Was he being tracked by this creature, this D'kourikai, instead of being stalked by it? Could it only see certain bits and pieces of his life and not the whole package? It was certainly possible, and perhaps even more likely. It didn't make sense.

"You see? How could I know all this and it be one big coincidence?" Jennifer offered. Her tone of voice was becoming more certain, more pronounced. "You can act like you know more than me, or you can open up and work with me. The choice is yours, John."

Very slowly, a look of acceptance developed on his once-doubtful face. This girl was a natural intuitive. She had a protective instinct about her, a look of power behind her black eyes.

"Thank you for believing me." She smiled.

"Hey, as long as you keep the monsters out, I guess it's fine. I don't mean to kick you out now, but I've had a long day and I am exhausted."

"That's okay. Will you take me to the house on Mayberry Road tomorrow?"

"No. Good-night."

"Good-night." She turned, disappointed.

She left and closed the door behind her as John jumped into bed, laced his hands behind his head, and tried to clear his jumbled mind.

***

A little later, before turning in for good, John went outside and found Lucky lying beside a fire hydrant near Stover Street. He fed him a few treats and snuck him back into his room. He shut off the bedside lamp and the cell phone, opened the window from which the new dream catcher hung, got into bed, and pet Lucky on his belly. He eased into sleep, the previous thoughts of the day scattering away. In no time, he left the conscious world behind.

The night passed slowly, calmly, unheedingly, and neither John nor Lucky changed position in bed. A soothing wind blew in through the window with a dull, bassy roar. Jennifer's dream catcher swayed from side to side. A full moon hung low over the rolling hills in the distance. Serenity had come to Bellsville.

***

In his dream, he saw a woman's small, wrinkled hands snip off strands of hair with a pair of scissors. Her blurred face shifted in the background in slow motion. The hair strands feathered to the floor.

"Find help, Mary," the foreign female voice echoed through John's ears.

A dustpan dropped to a black and white checkerboard floor, and a small broom swept the hair up into it. The person doing the cleaning entered the light and finally became visible in John's eyes. It was an older woman with serious, almond shaped eyes, and a face riddled with trench-like acne scars. *A very familiar face*, he thought, even though he could not place it. He didn't know her, but he had seen her before...but when?

Then, another voice echoed through his ears, its tone louder and more critical—his mother's.

The visual composition of the barbershop scene changed. The floor, the hair, and the hairdresser were replaced by clouds, a golden light, and a pretty blue sky. His mother floated forward across thin air without moving a single foot. She was dressed like an angel again, clad in white clothes, her face, in contrast, weighed with concern.

She suddenly vanished.

Standing on a cloud and afraid to glance down, John looked around for her. She was nowhere to be seen.

"Get a haircut, kid! Tomorrow. Do not wait," she demanded, reappearing right before him, causing him to stumble backward, startled. Her message resounded over and over, its tone infused with utmost urgency.

Again, she vanished, along with her the clouds, the golden light, and the blue sky. Darkness washed over him. Soon, small specs of light burned to life in the distance, filling the void. He was staring up at the night sky. He could not move, could not speak when he tried. He was bound to the earth and granted only the ability to watch and listen.

It was the *feeling* he felt that really caught his attention. Something was burrowing through the heavens, coming for him, after him. It was infuriated with his constant attempt to shield *It* away. It didn't exactly fly. It didn't exactly float. It used the earth's atmosphere as a ground to walk on. It was hungry, and had been so for many years. It was coming for him tonight, now, to break down the object that shunned it away.

The dream catcher fluttered amidst the increasingly cool

wind. John licked his lips as he slept. Lucky's ears rose and his eyes opened. He looked up at the relic hanging from the window as it undulated in a strange manner, as if something more than just the wind was affecting it.

The dog whimpered. Scratched at John's arm. Barked.

The webs of the dream catcher broke apart one by one. The feathers on its outside edges fell off and fluttered to the windowsill. The wooden frame blackened, smoked, and burst into flames.

It went up as if it had been doused in gasoline and set ablaze by a blowtorch. D'kourikai had come to shatter John's mental blockade:

The dream catcher.

D'kourikai was not about to submit to such an artifact, especially made from some vile human—the same race who was long ago indirectly responsible for imprisoning Cthulhu.

Not only did the dream catcher go up in flames, but the whole windowsill did as well...along with the curtain, the walls, the ceiling. D'kourikai breathed fire from its mouth. Lucky could see the outline of the entity, but that was all. He began barking violently at it, at the flames, and at his owner, trying to wake him.

John slept through everything, immersed in darkness and imprisoned mentally by the fire-breathing monster, which had locked him out of consciousness. He had no way of waking up for the time being—even as the upper apartments caught fire or as people in the other rooms began screaming and panicking. The fire department had arrived before John had any idea what was going on.

By some miracle, the smoke had not killed him. Yet.

John's room was clouded in blackness, soot filling every crevice and corner. Lucky struggled to breathe, but tried persistently and relentlessly to wake his master by barking in his ear or by biting his arm. Still, he wouldn't wake, even though he was beginning to suffocate.

Standing at the very back of his mind was his mother. She was trying to say something to him, but he could not make out the faint mumble of her words.

"John. Wa—p. Get ou—before it's t—late."

"Mom? Moooom! I can't hear you!" he shouted.

"John!" she said, trying to get closer, trying to speak louder. It wasn't happening.

All of a sudden, the rough, unrecognizable shape of a young girl materialized from out of the vortex of fog, and shouted, *"John, you have to wake up! The building's on fire!"*

He was up in a flash, enshrouded by smoke and unable to see so much as his hand in front of his face. The walloping sound of fire truck sirens filled his ears, reviving him completely from his slumber.

He jumped to his feet with Lucky by his side and went to where he thought the door was. He slipped twice, once on a magazine and once on a remote control. His hand managed to find the doorknob almost by itself, but he yanked it away from the scorching brass before it had a chance to burn. The metal was glowing, a red hot, semitransparent knob John could not see. It was being bombarded by flames from the opposite side.

"Shit."

Panicked, Lucky began to spin around in circles and howl desperately. Like John, he was on the verge of falling over due to a lack of oxygen. John turned and looked for the window. It was pointless. The black smoke masked everything in view. He did not have time to search for it without passing out and likely dying. So, instead, he kicked at the door with the heel of his foot, over and over, hoping he had the time to jump aside before the backdraft crashed into the room.

"Breeeeaaak! Goddamn you, break!"

Thigh muscles throbbing, John quickly realized that his attempt at kicking the door wasn't working. Lucky stopped circling and sprawled out on the floor. The crackling of flames now accompanied the whaling of the trucks outside.

There was an enormous crash, and much of the smoke fanned out of the room, long enough for John and Lucky to take in a few deep breaths of cleaner air. John could suddenly see and realized that he and his dog were actually still alive. His room had changed. His ceiling was gone and was now just a gaping hole. Sections of the floor above had weakened and given out, toppling down to his level. The sight he saw, however, was one he would have traded in for anything.

Atop his bigger bed lay a smaller one in which an elderly woman lay, engulfed in flames. Her once-gray hair was gone, singed down to the roots. He couldn't bear the smell of her burning flesh. But worse than the smell was the expression on her desperate, horrified face as she lay there, powerless and desperate, her eyes melting away.

He had to help her. He could not stand watching an innocent elderly woman die, especially this way. He felt like he was at fault yet again for another person's unnecessary death. He stepped forward to help the woman. As he did, he heard the voice of his mother say *No, John, there's no time. You cannot help her.*

He stepped forward again, anyway. Lucky lunged down, bit his pant leg, and tugged him back toward the door, which was now beginning to bulge inwardly.

"I have to save her!" John shouted.

No, son, you got to go now!

John reached for the woman. More flames engulfed her. She reached for him, too, mouthing the words *help me.*

Just then, an explosion burst through the room, and fragments of the door scattered through the window, into the bathroom, into the wall, and against John's body, knocking him down. Lucky scratched at his leg. Barked until John was back on his feet, and then nodded to the door, telling him to follow.

I have to help this woman first.

John! His mother raised her voice.

"I have to help—" He looked back at the old woman. She was no longer struggling or whimpering. She was dead.

I failed again.

A tear welled in his eye, but before it fell, he, along with Lucky, were gone from the room.

He wasn't as much focused on escape as he was on the fact that he had wasted too much time and let the woman perish. He followed Lucky through the dense, choking black smoke in the hall and past the intense, unbearable heat, neither of which registered in his preoccupied mind. He hurried toward the exit—or where he thought the exit was—hardly concerned with his own mortality.

Solid hard objects obstructed the path, and there was no visibility whatsoever. People screamed. Fire crackled. Sirens echoed through the hall. John stumbled forward, coughing. Lucky guided him over the rubble. Still, he almost tripped a dozen times in only a few strides. To better support himself, he reached out with his hand and leaned against a wall. Slowly, he edged his way along, wondering if his best friend was going the right way. He could barely breathe, he could not see, and his body was beading with sweat in response to the extreme heat. He had never been so hot. Some of the flames were red, yellow and orange, while others were purple, green, white, and blue.

"Lucky, hold on, I can't go so fast!" John pleaded, his

trembling hand losing contact with the wall. Lucky let go of his pant leg and howled, as if in pain.

"Are you all right?"

Lucky howled again. He was okay for the time being, but the dog knew that time was their great enemy right now. The smoke was killing them both. They had to hurry. And John was taking his good old time.

As they continued their way through the dark smoke, John saw a faint light up ahead. A flashlight. "I got you," a deep voice said as a pair of muscular arms wrapped around him. "You're going to be okay."

John didn't remember much of the next few minutes other than being pulled out of the building by a man in a yellow uniform. As soon as he joined the outside world, he could breathe again. The air was sweet. In his blurred vision, he saw people talking to him, laying him on a stretcher, and opening the back door of an ambulance, into which they lifted him.

This was the last thing he saw before he passed out.

***

John didn't wake until the following day, but when he did, he was alone in a hospital bed at Lecorrd Medical Center, well rested, with a dull throb in his head and a sharp pain in his lungs. The ultra-strong scent of bleach stinking up the room didn't help, nor did the bright shaft of sunlight shimmering in through the nearby window. He was comfortable, even though he wasn't sure if he should have been.

Innocents had perished. A building had been destroyed. He had almost died.

He wanted to be glad he was not dead, but he could not completely bring himself to be. He seemed to be cursed by D'kourikai. He could not escape It. It was probably watching

119

him now. John wasn't sure if there was any way to stop it.

There were two knocks on the door, tearing him from his thoughts.

He looked up. Jennifer was standing right outside the door, dressed in the same clothes as the day before, without so much as a mark on her.

"John?"

"Jennifer. Hi. Come in."

She stepped into the room and walked over to the bed, her hands clasped together in front of her. She looked nervous and strangely calm at once. She had to be hiding something.

"How did you—" he started.

"Luck, I guess. I received a call fifteen minutes before the fire broke out that my three-year-old niece tumbled down a flight of stairs. She got banged up pretty bad. Concussion. Broken bones. I've been here since last evening. The news came on when I was sitting in the waiting room. I couldn't believe it. I strongly believe I would have died in the fire if I hadn't left. Funny, huh? Someone else gets hurt and it saves my life."

"I should be dead too."

"That fire was meant for me, John. I put the dream catcher in your room. That despicable thing wanted *me* to die most of all. Why was *I* spared?"

"I don't know. I was spared just as much as you."

"If it wasn't for me, then all those people wouldn't have—almost everyone in that building died. A few were burnt alive. Do you know that besides you, me, and some teenage boy, all the others from that building are either dead or dying? There were over a hundred people in there."

John's eyes glazed over. Was it true? Was he one of only three people to have left that building practically uninjured?

Jennifer bowed her head. "And by trying to help you, I

ended up taking the lives of all my neighbors. Life's so ironic."

He knew exactly how she felt. He was just as responsible as she thought she was, if not more.

Too many people had died thus far, period. Not just those in the United Apartments, but others at the house on Mayberry Road. He was in a war he could not win.

"It is not your fault, Jennifer," he said, more to himself, and more doubtful than truthful. "You have no control over life or death."

"My action caused death."

"You didn't know *that* would happen."

Tears welled in her eyes. She forced them away. John changed the subject to try to make her feel better: "Is Lucky okay?"

She finally smiled. "Yeah, he's fine. We took him to my cousin's house. He's just like a person." She paused for a second to catch her breath, then said something that caught him off guard: "Can you take me to the house on Mayberry Road?"

His eyes lit up. He almost gasped, trying to summon a response. His mind was blank. "When?"

"Soon. When you get out of here. I have to see it for myself. It's been an obsession."

"That's exactly why you shouldn't go near it!"

She interrupted: "I must have the—"

He interrupted her before she could finish: "Yes, you will. Soon. But understand that when you do enter, you're under my instruction the entire time. No arguments, no being curious or brave."

"You have my word." Then she said, "Have you heard about the lunar eclipse tonight?"

John shook his head, unsure if he wanted to hear the

answer.

"Nobody knew about it till just days ago. Astronomers said something about this particular event has not happened in centuries. Meteor showers and visible lights in the sky over many parts of the world, like the Aurora Borealis, but visible as far south as Pensacola. One person said they thought they discovered a new planet within our solar system. I have a feeling that the thing in the house on Mayberry Road has something to do with it, whether it's causing it or waiting for it."

"How do you know that?"

"Just a feeling."

John's eyes moved. He looked over Jennifer's shoulder. A young man who could have been her brother was standing outside the room in the dimly-lit hallway.

"Jen?" the unknown man said.

She turned. A big smile appeared on her face, as if she hadn't seen the man in years. "Patrick! Hey!"

She turned back to John. "Hey, I'm sorry, but I gotta run. I will see you tomorrow for sure. Be well, my new friend." Jennifer left the room, hugged the man and pecked him on the lips. John felt a pang of jealousy as he realized this man must be her husband. He watched as she and he got reacquainted and walked away, leaving him alone.

CHAPTER TWELVE

John laid there for a while, staring out the window and up at the beautiful, cloudless sky. The sun was huge, low, its rays warming his legs. A flock of geese flew over the Ohio River, toward the rolling hills. He heard almost no sound, except for the occasional car horn from outside or the hospital intercom calling for a missing doctor. For once, he was in a peaceful state of mind. He knew moments like this were rare—natural spiritual meditation—when he didn't have to consciously meditate to block or filter impeding thoughts. They simply went away on their own without any explanation at all.

"Mr. Rollings?" The voice distracted him. A woman entered the room, food tray in hand.

His taste of nirvana was gone. He broke from his hypnotic trance and joined the world. *Thanks, lady.*

The woman, an overweight black woman with weaves in her hair and a big gap between her front teeth, walked over to her patient and set the food tray down on his lap. He looked at the goods: a turkey sandwich, a cup of applesauce, a pint of low-fat milk.

He started digging in right away.

"So, how are you doing? You breathed in a lot of smoke, you know? Luckily you didn't get burned. Somebody was looking out for you up there."

John snickered and ate. "I wish that was always so. Can't win them all."

"Let's get your blood pressure here." She grabbed the blood pressure cuff off the wall and wrapped it around his left arm. John swallowed some applesauce.

Ting-ting. The woman knocked something to the floor.

"Whoops," she said, reaching down for...a *scalpel.* Suddenly, her voice changed, and turned so horrible that John choked on his food.

"You can't win them all, Rock a bye Rollings!" It came from her mouth, but it wasn't *her* voice. It was D'kourikai's.

John jerked his head aside. The woman jolted upright and put the scalpel against his throat. Her face had changed, had transformed into a bloody, red, lumpy, disease-stricken monster that smelled like rotting flesh. John had seen photos of people stricken with smallpox and photos of victims who had hemorrhaged from Ebola. This looked like both of those combined into one grotesque manifestation. Yet, he couldn't help but stare.

"Last night was a taste of what I can do. I can pluck your soul from your body like feathers off a chicken. You defend against another of my dreams, and I will cut your head off."

John's thoughts went to Jennifer. He wanted to see if this thing was all-powerful. "Jennifer? You tried to kill her, didn't you?"

The possessed woman looked confused. Blood popped from her boils like puss. Thinner blood leaked down from her eyes.

"She needed to die in flames!"

But was that the truth? There was a moment's hesitation before it had answered, or was that just his imagination?

The evil behind those bleeding eyes suddenly vanished as

D'kourikai disappeared, leaving behind a pained woman with two very deadly diseases in her body. Blood oozed and spurted from every facial orifice. Blood beaded from her pores. A clump of hair tore out of her scalp.

When she parted her lips to speak, three of her teeth came out and fell to the floor. One of her eyes bulged from its socket, its surface covered with small, wart-like bumps. The blood continued to come, then began to literally *pour* down from her face with the consistency of water. She whimpered and reached for John, who only backed away, frightened. The skin on her extended hand cracked, bled, and peeled. Every fingernail fell off. Vomit, filled with bits of internal organs, barely missed him. He doubled over, nearly vomiting himself.

At last, she stumbled, fell onto her back, and began trembling violently. John watched, repulsed. Once on the floor, her body immediately went limp.

"Jesus-H-Christ! What happened here?" exclaimed another nurse entering the room.

John could not speak, at first. When he did, the most bizarre combination of words exited his mouth: "I need a haircut."

***

He got to leave—later—after answering a bunch of questions he didn't really have answers to. He said nothing about D'kourikai. to the police. He didn't say much of anything. Steera mentioned to them that John was working a vitally important case and needed to be able to leave on his own cognizance. So, at 3:04 in the afternoon, he dressed and left the hospital to go get a trim at his usual barber: Mary Ann's.

Sheriff Steera was his de facto chauffeur since John's car was still at the apartment building. "Well, I've got some bad news about that one, son," Steera said after John inquired about his car. "It was damaged pretty heavily in the fire. I think it might actually be in a junk yard at this point. I hope you were fully insured."

Choosing not to carry a renter's policy or full coverage on the vehicle, he had only driver's liability insurance, insurance that wouldn't cover any vehicle damage caused by an apartment fire. He wasn't too concerned, however. He had more important things to worry about.

"I'll just wait out here for you," Steera said as he stopped in front of the Mary Ann's Barber Shop. "My sister works here, you know."

"You don't say. That's cool. I haven't been here since I was a boy. I'll say 'hi' for you."

"Make sure you tip her well."

After Steera let him out of the car, John walked up to the building. It was an older place, its brick walls covered in ugly graffiti, one of its front partitions cracked slightly in its upper corner. But the lights were on, a "WE'RE OPEN" sign hung in the door window, and people were inside getting their hair cut.

A loud clap of thunder roared from above. He looked up, only to watch a large, direct bolt of lightning trail down from a black cloud, almost striking the roof of the barber shop. That was strange. This stormed seemed to come out of nowhere.

He entered the building, and the door closed behind him with a loud thud. A bell hanging overhead rang. Everyone inside turned to see who it was. The barbers halted in mid-trim. Four people were looking at him as if he had capsized one great party.

One of the two barbers, both of whom were woman—possibly Steera's sister—smiled. "Take a seat there, and I'll be with you shortly."

He quietly sat down and looked around the shop. The checkerboard floors, the many recesses in the walls, the antique mirrors—even the oily smell in the air—somehow reminded him of the house on Mayberry Road. John relaxed for a few moments, watching the breaking local news story on a small HDTV.

Jack Hillsmouth, probably the most well-known news anchor in the area (and sexiest according to most women within a hundred miles) was standing in front of the United Apartment Building that had burned to the ground last night, microphone in hand and a smug little smile on his face. The anchor didn't offer any details John didn't already know, including the fact that only three residents managed to survive.

"Okay, you ready?" the hairdresser said, smiling at John. He stood and got into the closest reclining chair. The woman tied a cloth around him and hooked it shut.

"How do you want your hair cut?"

"Uh, just a trim. Little off the sides. Not too much off the top."

"Okay. I gotcha." She grabbed a pair of scissors and went to work. John watched her in the mirror as she snipped and moved. She was most definitely Steera's sister. The eyes, the mouth, the hair color, the nose—everything.

"Your brother says 'hi,'" John made eye contact with her reflection.

"You know my brother?"

"He's the sheriff, right?"

"Yes, he is. So are you in law enforcement?"

"Not exactly."

"So what do you do, John?"

"I don't really do anything, really. I mean, I'm kind of a volunteer detective, you could say."

"That's so interesting. I've always wanted to do that. You know, cutting hair isn't exactly the most exciting job in the world. Oh, by the way, the name is Patricia Goldsmith."

"John Rollings."

She drew in a breath. It seemed almost as if she received an electric shock. "You."

As she stepped away, images flooded his mind. He saw Patricia, from an earlier decade and of a much younger age, sweeping hair into a dustpan, and then dumping it into a clear plastic sandwich bag before handing it to someone else, as if it contained something vitally important.

"My hair? Who did you give my hair to when I was a boy? You cut it and gave it to somebody. You put it in a plastic baggy...and—" He trailed off.

Patricia dropped the scissors.

John gazed at her reflection in the mirror. He thought the glass was going to break.

"You couldn't possibly remember that." Her voice was uneasy and tense. The other barbers and customers were now looking her way.

"I do remember. I just want to know who and why. Why did you save my hair for someone? Who did you give it to?"

She tried to speak again, but all that would form were small yelps in the back of her throat. She eventually got herself together. "I don't know what he wanted it for. That was when—"

"What?" John demanded. "When what?"

"When she—when Mary—"

"Who's Mary?" John pushed.

Tears gleamed in her eyes. "I don't know why my brother wanted your hair. He was confused and messed up at the time. He didn't give me an explanation. I just did it for him, thinking it was no big deal. Please, don't tell him I told you.

He would be so angry." She wiped away her watery eyes. To John, there was still much more to be discovered. And only one man held the answer: Charlie Steera.

John thought about asking Patricia another question, but decided it'd be best not to. She looked upset already, and he knew he would get a clearer answer from the sheriff's mouth.

John threw a twenty on the table and left the shop, and immediately hopped into Steera's car.

"John. Hey, tip her well like I asked?" John didn't respond. "You all right? Jesus, you look pale. She didn't cut your jugular, did she?" Charlie looked confused. "Is everything all right?"

"Charlie, what the hell did you need my hair for? I need to know now. No lies, no tales. The truth."

Charlie drooped his head, sighed, and rubbed his face harshly with one fat hand. "Shit. I didn't want you to find out. Not this way. I knew I should have taken you somewhere else…but my sister, she—"

"The truth." John stared him down.

"The truth. I wish someone could have told me that too." Steera took three deep breaths. This was the first time John had seen him utterly vulnerable.

"My wife, Mary…she needed my help. She disappeared when you were only a boy. I went to work one day and when I came home, she was gone without a trace. No leads, no witnesses, nothing. It's like she vanished off the face of the Earth. I turned this whole tri-state area upside down looking for clues or any evidence of her I could find. Then one day I was investigating a suspected drug house just off of Mayberry Road. The criminal saw me and took off running out the back door. I chased after him, through the woods, where I eventually lost him. That's when I came to that house on Mayberry Road. So I went inside on a hunch that *that's* where the man was hiding, perhaps waiting for me to move on and look elsewhere. At the time, I knew nothing of that terrible place. But as soon as I entered, the beast materialized before me. I couldn't move. I couldn't breathe. It somehow just *knew* about Mary. It knew things about her only she and I knew. Intimate details. It told me that it could track her for me, lead me right to her! I loved her so much. I said I would do anything. I made a deal with that monster. I would bring it a small, tangible specimen from a young male child. D'kourikai didn't tell me why it needed a child's DNA. God, I am so sorry. And that *fuck* lied to me! It never found Mary for me. It gave me bad dreams of what might have happened to her. When I threatened to burn that house down, it threatened to bring me into its world...its stifling world of true hell. I did nothing after that. I could do nothing. But it needs you to survive. I need you to help me kill it. You're the only one. I think it's afraid of you. Do you see now why I asked you to help me?"

"Why hasn't it attacked you since we've started?" John's mouth began to pucker.

After a moment's hesitation, he said, "I don't pose a threat. It thinks I'm too weak to do anything."

"*Nobody* who's gone in there has posed a threat."

"That's because it's trying to show us who's boss. It wants us to be afraid."

Silence fell between the two men. Neither of them spoke or looked at each other for a while. Nothing much else could be said. John was still absorbing the information. It was like trying to digest his grandmother's meatloaf. It took time, patience, and maybe a few tums, which, in this case, may have been a long period of meditation or escape from the truth.

"John, I know you don't have a place to stay. You are

more than welcome to live at my house until you figure things out."

"No. That's my problem, not yours."

"It's no trouble at all. Really. Besides, I could use some company."

John gazed downward, indifferent. "I will find my own place, Charlie. But thanks. I have a friend I haven't seen in a while who moved back in town not long ago. I may stay with him."

"Okay. Well, the offer stands if you change your mind."

The sheriff sat silent for a moment as if he wanted to ask John a favor, but was afraid to. After several awkward seconds, he finally spoke, "John, can you find Mary for me? Is there any way you can see where she is? What happened to her?"

"What? How would I be able to do that?"

CHAPTER THIRTEEN

Later that day, during the onset of dusk, Steera dropped John off at the home of an old friend in the neighboring town of Leccord. John stepped into a small shaft of reflected blue streetlight. He was standing on a concrete porch, where a wooden swing lay in a broken heap back by the far railing. A rusty mailbox hung from one screw beside a cracked screen door. John checked the address on it again—1609 Chestnut Street—just to make sure he was at the right place. He was, but there were no lights on in the windows. There was no sound from within. No one appeared to be home.

A noise eventually sounded from behind the front door, and an outside light burned to life. John stepped back just as the main door swung open and the stingy odor of cigarette smoke entered his lungs.

Yep, this is the right place. Ben Krambers.

"Well, you're not dead, after all," John said with a grin. Ben, who was completely bald, bone-thin, and ravaged-looking, removed a lit Camel from his lips.

"Do I know you…wait—*John?*"

"In the flesh."

Ben removed the cigarette from his lips. "Jesus, man, how the hell you doing? I haven't seen your ugly mug since high school!"

"Has it really been that long? Seems like only three or four years."

"Hell, I don't know. Well anyway, come in, come in."

John had never known a soul outside his family as long as he had known Ben, who had been there for him through all the bullying at school. Both men had little in common, had different opinions on many things, and had lived different lifestyles. Regardless, they were like brothers, or had been at one time. "You look good, man. I figured you would have been possessed or something by now." Ben coughed and invited him in and then closed the door.

"Take a seat," Ben said. "Oh, and excuse the mess. I had to fire my maid. She was stealing my trash."

The living room wasn't a mess, it was an abomination. The carpeted floor was sticky where it wasn't littered with mounds of trash or dirty clothes. Newspapers were randomly placed over spots where his cat had peed or pooped (as Ben would explain later). The walls were cracked, and the ceiling was ripped open where the roof was leaking. A bucket sat in the center of the room to collect the water. However, the odors were almost worse than the sights. It was so unbearable that John could barely keep from vomiting. Urine, fecal matter, rotten food, and cigarette smoke were all mixed together.

Great, he thought, *this is my new stay.*

John sat on an ugly, lumpy couch. His friend sat across from him in a rocking chair and lit another smoke. Ben's hands were shaky, unsteady, quite unlike the ones John remembered during childhood. His face was rough, ragged, blemished. He didn't look early-thirties, he looked like he was in his fifties.

What happened to you, Ben?

"Sorry I didn't contact you sooner." John looked down, away from Ben. "I meant to."

"Oh, don't worry about it." Ben waved his bony hand. "You're here now. I've only been back for a year, anyway. I know you've been busy. I have been, too."

"What have you been doing?" John suddenly wished he hadn't asked that question.

"Well..." He thought about it. "I finally souped up my Hemi. Runs awesome now. We'll have to cruise sometime."

John nodded and looked around the disorganized room. "That's nice. You ever go back to school? Get your diploma?"

Ben got quiet. His eyes glowed like the cherry on his cigarette.

John held up his hands. "I'm sorry, man. I didn't mean to dredge up old memories."

Ben flicked some ashes onto his carpet and rubbed them in with his heel. "Oh, it's okay. I'm over it. We haven't seen each other since when? Eleventh grade?"

"Yeah, when you...quit."

"I don't consider what I did as *quitting*. School just wasn't for me. I always saw myself as a freelancer doing whatever job I wanted depending on how I felt. Now I make my money off the government."

"How?"

"Disability."

John hated hearing that. His old friend was in even worse shape than he'd originally predicted.

"You still into digital photography?"

Ben sucked in on his Camel. "No way, man. It's a waste of time and energy. I haven't done that forever. Nobody buys shit like that anymore. Not even on Ebay. You gotta go to college for that and you know how little I like school."

John could only shake his head.

"It's a shame your placed burned down and all. You lived there for a while, didn't you?"

John nodded.

Ben shook his head and finished his cigarette. "Well, I'm glad to have you here. Wish the circumstances were different." He coughed.

John looked again at the mess. Without even looking at him, Ben explained, "Yeah, I know what you're thinking, John. You feel sorry for me. You think I'm a bum. A waste. A loser. A piece of scum who never achieved anything in life because I was selfish and lazy. I've never even kissed a girl before, just as you said would happen when we were teens. I'm always going to be alone, just as you predicted. Sometimes I ask myself if I would be somewhere else, someone better, if I hadn't heard what you told me back then. Maybe if we'd never known each other I would be a famous photographer."

John looked heartbroken. "Ben, I'm sorry. Whatever I said when we were—"

Ben interrupted: *"Don't* be sorry! You were right. Everything you said, you were right. Even the lung cancer."

John swallowed hard. "What? Are you sure?"

"Yes. Three opinions. They say they can try to help me with Chemo, but it's so far advanced now that they don't think it'll really help all that much. I'm days away from dying, John." As if to accentuate that point, he doubled over in a fit of coughing. When he recovered, Ben said, "I don't want to be helped or saved."

"Ben, listen, maybe there's a way. Some doctor in—"

Ben interrupted him again. "No. As I said, I don't wanna be saved. If there's half a chance of there being a better world than this, as you used to say—Heaven—I want to go there. That's the place where all my dreams will come true. That's where I want to be."

"So you're giving up? Just like that?"

"What do you want me to do? You want me to show you what I cough up in the sink when I wake up? That I can't breathe when I'm lying there trying to sleep? That I—*fucking hate life!*" Ben shoved a slew of empty beer cans off a nearby stand. John didn't flinch.

"Heaven, Ben, is where you go after you complete your journey. You haven't even started yet."

"But God wants to end me." Ben pointed to his cigarette and stamped it out.

"You made some bad choices. We all do. You can't let a few bad choices derail you for good."

"Oh yeah? Well, I can't turn back time, can I?"

John was silent.

"That's what I thought. Hell, Heaven isn't gonna take me, anyway. I'm fucked. Always have been. Nobody was ever there for me...to help me."

"No. *You* were never there for you. I tried to help you, but you didn't want to hear my advice. It's the same story with everyone else who lent you their helping hand. You think your way is better than everyone else's. You're stubborn. You were since I first met you, but don't throw in the towel! I don't care if you're coughing blood and can't breathe. Sometimes you have to say fuck it and live, regardless. You're like my brother. If you're dying, you're dying, but don't be weak and say the hell with it. There are others who aren't dying and say that very same thing. When we were kids, you never gave up playing guitar … until you became a teenager and a few people said you weren't any good. Fuck them all, Ben. Believe in yourself, not the negativity. You should do what you want to do regardless of how good or bad you are at it. Do it for you, not for them."

"What should I do then? I feel like I'm in a place I can't escape from."

"We're all there. It's called Earth. I'm going to ask of you a favor."

"Anything."

John clasped his hands together and drew a breath. "I need some money, if you can loan it to me. I lost quite a few things in that fire, and I wasn't insured. I need to buy some clothes and other essentials. Now, in return for that money, I'm buying your cancer from you. I'm also buying your worries and fears and bad experiences."

Ben looked extremely confused. He almost laughed. *"What?* I tell you I'm dying and on disability, and you ask me for money?"

"It's not like that, Ben. You don't dwell on any bullshit until I return your money back to you. You don't think about dying, or any pain, and you don't complain at all."

Ben managed a laugh between coughs. "That's a tall order, but...deal."

They shook hands and laughed at the sheer ridiculousness of the situation.

***

John slept soundly that night. He slept in the darkness of his mind, in the darkness of Ben's living room, slowly drifting into a white mist somewhere in a great expanse of utter nothingness. The mist thickened, and then diffused into a gentle fog. A bright, yet soothing, gold light followed it, burning the darkness away. John could feel its warmth against his body. A figure approached—appeared—from the mist, dressed in a gown so white it looked unusual. He could not make out any features of the person, except that she had flowing brown hair. The woman floated toward him, the light behind her dispersing into lasers. Her face became visible. It was gentle, happy, kind, and utterly unfamiliar. John had never seen her before in his life, but she bore a faint resemblance to depictions of Mary, the mother of God."

Then she spoke to him without moving her mouth: "John…." She smiled. The light behind her grew brighter. Her emerald eyes became greener.

John posed a question. "Who are you?" He was standing in a dark space, not at the entrance to heaven, as was she.

"I am Mary."

He immediately bowed before her in show of reverence.

"John, you needn't do that."

"But aren't you Jesus's mother?"

"No, John, nothing quite so grand."

"But you look like her."

"Coincidence, John. Nothing more. I need your help in finding my killer. I was murdered before my time. Something is blocking my view of seeing who killed me, so I need earthly help. I need your help to find the one who did it and imprison him before he does something else." She smiled again. A gentle breeze ruffled her almost-opaque form.

"How will I find him?"

"I have but one clue I am able to see."

An image—an extreme close up—of a small, black-inked Grim-Reaper tattoo on a man's arm or leg appeared in the mist. The texture and hairiness confirmed it was a male, but even that was uncertain.

Then, the projected image was gone, except for the new imprint in John's mind. The light began to dissolve away afterward, along with the woman, the mist.

"Wait!" He reached for her. She was receding quickly, now barely a shadow.

"I have faith in you that you will find him. And by the way, *do not* go into that house again without orange juice."

"Wait! Are you Charlie Steera's wife?"

The woman disappeared without answering.

***

John woke the next morning to the sight of Ben standing over him, a cigarette in one hand, a slice of pizza in the other. He was chewing loudly. Daylight shined through the stained-glass windows in little rainbows. Outside, children laughed as they ran home from school.

"Want a slice of pizza? It's got everything on it, with extra anchovies." Ben extended him a slice.

"No thanks. What time is it?"

"Suit yourself. It's a little after three, you lazy ass. Time to get up." Ben sat down in his chair and stuffed a pizza in his mouth.

"Nice lunch there, huh? I see you never gave up pizza."

"Hey, it's my favorite. Papa John's is only three blocks away. I think it pisses them off when I tell them to deliver it. Not to mention I'm a shitty tipper."

John chuckled and shook his head.

The shrilling wail of a cell phone rang through the room. Ben reached over, picked it up, and opened it.

The display read: *Unknown Caller.*

He put the phone to his ear. "Hello?"

"Hello, is John there?" Jennifer's voice blared through the receiver.

"Uh, yeah, hold on." Ben tossed him the phone. "It's some chick."

John caught it and put it to his ear. "Hello?"

"Hey! Where are you? I went to the E.R. and they said you left. Yesterday. I was scared something happened to you."

"Nope. I'm alive and well."

John got up and walked out the front door. Once outside, he sat on the step and looked forward. "How'd you get this number?"

"The digits came to me in a dream. I almost didn't call, but the urge wouldn't let me alone. Are you still seeing...It?"

"No, actually I haven't. Not since yesterday."

"Okay, good. I didn't think you would anymore. Not for a while anyway." She sounded grateful.

"What do you mean? Have you seen something?" John was curious.

"No, not recently. But I would like to meet up with you today. I do have to talk to you. Can you meet me at Piper's Cafe? Say, in an hour?"

"I don't have a car. I'm not even in Bellsville right now."

"Can you get a cab? I'll pay for the fair when you meet me there."

"Are you sure? I mean—"

She interrupted, "Please. It'd be my pleasure. Four o' clock."

"Fine, I'll be there."

"Great! See you then." She hung up. John did too.

He looked up at the sky, at a blistering bright sun. It radiated the same warmth he felt only moments ago in the dream. Beyond the orange round sphere was nothing but seas of blue, scattered with hints of departing clouds. He wanted to believe his mother was looking down at him, smiling, proud of her only child. Maybe she was. Maybe she was standing by his side with her hand on his shoulder.

***

A dented cab pulled up to a city curb at 3:59 P.M. Jennifer was already standing on the sidewalk by a fire hydrant, dressed in a pretty green dress and holding a blood-red purse on her skinny arm. She smiled and waved at John before the dirty yellow vehicle came to a complete stop. He rolled down his window as she approached.

"That'll be twenty-two dollars, sir," the cab driver barked, as if John intended to jump out without paying.

Twenty-two, John thought. He did not like that number.

Jennifer came over and handed the money to the smelly, overweight cabby. Then John got out, and barely had the chance to shut the door before the taxi peeled off down the road.

"You know I could have paid him." John gave her the look. "Dinner is definitely on me."

"We'll see."

John followed her into the small restaurant. He had heard good things of the place, but had never actually stepped foot inside the building. Supposedly their burgers were to die for. Their soups, too, were highly recommended by many locals. A large sign in the doorway announced their daily special: Chicken Alfredo with salad and garlic bread. The place was alive with conversation.

A stick-thin waitress with a big mole on her cheek welcomed them in and led them to a booth by the window. They sat.

"Here are your menus. May I get you something to drink?"

Jennifer cleared her scratchy throat. "Water."

"Tea," John requested.

"Okay, I'll be right back with your drinks." The waitress smiled and walked away.

John opened his menu and browsed the selection. "I hope your husband doesn't find you dining with another guy."

She fumblingly opened her menu, flustered by what he just said. "Oh, he's not like that. My husband won't—*isn't*—jealous."

Her disarranged sentence spawned an assault of curiosity in his mind. *Why did she accidentally say...?*

She set down the menu and spoke, this time much more articulately: "You said you slept okay last night? No bad dreams? Do you feel like it still has a lock on you?"

John set down his menu. "Why do you ask? What do you know?"

"Check your pocket."

John lowered his eyebrows, confused. He reached into his right pocket. Something was in there that he hadn't put there, that shouldn't have been there. Whatever it was, he pulled it out. It was a little purple leaf with a yellow stem.

"What the—"

Jennifer smiled thoughtfully. "It's wolfsbane. It's supposed to work like a dream catcher, but is more powerful. Some witches use it to confuse evil spirits so they can't be easily found by them. It's much like turning off a tracking device. I thought it might help sever the connection between you and It."

John examined the leaf. He could feel a subtle, yet strong energy emanating from it.

"It only works on two conditions. One, it loses its effect once it's completely shriveled up and dead."

"And the other?"

"It must be no more than four feet away from your body at any given time."

"But when I was in the hospital yesterday—when I was in bed, the nurse transformed into—"

"I slipped it into your pants pocket. Your jeans weren't exactly near your bed. You were still wearing the hospital gown. That leaf is almost dead, too. I have more in my car. My aunt grows them. Also, be careful handling it, as it's not exactly nonpoisonous. Make sure you wash your hands after touching it."

"Well, that's reassuring." He smiled. "You're something

else, Jennifer. If it weren't for you, I could be dead now, you know."

She smiled and played with her wedding ring.

Why does she have to be married, he thought with a mixture of lust and guilt.

The waitress set two drinks down on the table. "Are we ready to order?"

They were. They both ordered the special. The mole-faced girl walked away.

"Is Lucky okay?" John rubbed his hands together to warm them up.

"Yeah. He goes through soooo much food. Eats like a pig. I can see he misses you though. He always wants to go with me when I leave. Sometimes he whimpers."

John sipped on his tea. "I miss him, too. I think even Lucky is linked to me somehow, except in a good way."

Jennifer took a drink of water. "So, do you still think that house has the all-seeing eye?"

"No. I'm positive it doesn't. That's something you need to know. Charlie Steera—the sheriff who's been working with me—took a lock of my hair when I was a child and gave it to D'kourikai. His wife went missing one day. He made a deal with it to find her."

"Did it find her?"

"No. It tricked him. It lied to him. But I'm starting to believe that It has a weakness, whatever that may be. I don't know what it is yet, but I'm going to find it. If this leaf can break the connection, then who knows?" John began to fiddle with his straw. "I know what it wants."

"What's that?" Jennifer was very interested.

"It needs me to puncture the barrier between dimensions. It wants to become earthbound. It needs me, for whatever reason, to do so. The portal—that house—is already partly open. If it accomplishes what it intends, I have no idea what will happen or what it's capable of doing. It could collapse time and space, for all I know. We have to find out everything we can about the source of it all before we can fix anything. I get a sense that it was purposely created."

"Have you been in the basement? Usually things like this originate from below ground."

"That's what I was thinking. I'll go down there tomorrow."

"You mean *we'll* go down there."

He gave her a stern look. "No, not yet. It's not safe. If you go in, you're not coming out. It tried killing you in that fire because you were helping me. Now that it can't track me, I'm sure it's really pissed off at both of us now."

"But, John, I have to—"

John held up his hand. His face became more serious. "Jennifer, I get a bad feeling when I think about you going into that house. I know you want to embark on some spiritual adventure, but this is seriously dangerous. You're not going, and that's end of story. You gotta promise me."

Jennifer gazed into his eyes. Her face turned red. "No. I can't promise that."

"If you don't, then I'll just tell Charlie. You'll be in jail while he and I investigate."

"On what charge?"

"I don't know. Obstructing a police investigation? Trespassing? I'm sure he'll be able to come up with something that would stick for at least a few days, anyway."

"You would do that to me? After all I've done to help you?"

"I appreciate everything you've done for me. And for that, I don't want something terrible to happen to you. I'm doing this for your own good."

She sat back and sighed. Her flushed face slowly turned white again. "Whatever you say, John. I am going in there *sometime*, though. Maybe not tomorrow, but I will eventually."

John wanted to protest further, but didn't.

The waitress soon brought them their meals: two steaming bowls of pasta, a huge bowl of garden salad, and a platter of garlic bread sticks smothered with butter. They ate, delving into a new, lighter conversation that didn't include the topics of death, horror, or a particular house located minutes away.

***

John woke up the following day on Ben's couch, fully roused, with five new wolfsbanes stuffed in his pocket. He was not taking any chances. He made sure to get them from Jennifer the day before. She was very helpful despite her being mildly frustrated with him at Piper's Diner. Ben appeared to be gone. The house was quiet, warm, and stinky with the odors of old piss, cigarette smoke, and rotten food. John missed the smell of his old apartment, the color of the walls, and the way the sun came in through the window.

I'll miss Ben soon, John thought to himself. It almost brought a tear to his eye. Cigarettes and lungs were like a loaded gun with a happy trigger finger, and his friend was about to die from it.

John knew he needed to call Steera and head to the Mayberry House.

"I'm on my way to pick you up. Be there in a second," Charlie said and hung up.

Suddenly thirsty, John headed into the kitchen, flicked on the overhead, and opened the fridge. It was packed full of Miller, Budweiser, Vodka, and Smirnoff. The grills were sticky with spilled, rancid-smelling beer. There was no soda, water, or milk. The only thing without alcohol in it was a carton of orange juice. Probably for his Vodka.

John picked it up, opened the lid, and smelled it, just to make sure it wasn't spiked. It seemed normal. He took a long drink, downing almost sixteen ounces in one giant gulp. The liquid flowed coolly down his throat and into his stomach. Something about the taste of oranges triggered a fuzzy feeling in him. He remembered something about...*orange juice?*

John looked at the carton and made the vain attempt at clearing his mind. Like those bolts of lightning the other day, it hit him.

Mary came to me in a dream and told me not to go in the house on Mayberry Road again without orange juice.

He shook his head and laughed, thinking he was going crazy. It sounded too silly, too outlandish.

He absentmindedly looked aside. His eyes focused on a small, empty, unlabeled pill bottle sitting on the windowsill behind the faucet, just waiting to be filled.

John did just that. He filled the bottle to the top with orange juice and capped it. After he slipped it into his unoccupied right pocket, a car horn sounded from out front. It was from Chester County Sheriff's vehicle.

Ben's house was lifeless a moment later.

***

Charlie apologized to John multiple times during the drive to the house. John brushed him off until they came to a stop in the bare clearing; there, he sucked in his anger and decided to forget the past. "It's okay. What's done is done, Charlie. We all make mistakes. I've done things I wish I could change, too. Don't worry about it."

Life returned to the sheriff's eyes.

Both men stepped from the vehicle. Only John's eyes shot to the upper windows of the house. He felt closely watched and resented now that he was untraceable. He also had a bad feeling that not only could he be killed today, but that his soul could be sucked into some horrible alternate reality. There were many more things he didn't know about the house and D'kourikai than what he actually did. Figuring out the old-fashioned building thirty yards away was like an ancient caveman finding and playing with plutonium.

"Welcome, Mr. Rollings." Vaul appeared, hands folded behind back. He looked less like a mannequin today and more like a person with human expression.

John turned and looked around. There were far more soldiers and investigators here today than any previous time. Two plainly-dressed gentlemen were setting up some kind of bizarre, futuristic-looking contraption near the northeast window. Attached atop its three thin, curved lead rods was a latex balloon, which was floating high in the air. Three other young soldiers were busy setting up a large radar antenna, its topmost point aimed directly toward the front of the house. Tables stacked with new monitors and imagining equipment were everywhere, each one occupied by more soldiers, male and female. There had to have been fifty or more people standing or sitting, each doing a different job. John wanted to laugh at the scenario. He knew they would get the right information they wanted *only* if D'kourikai *wanted* to give it to them. That hadn't really happened yet.

I wonder if it can see me here, now, or if the wolfsbane still blinds it....

But he could feel the eyes watching him, furious, frustrated, beckoning him. He knew he was going in alone this time. He would not allow anyone else to follow him, lest they would die some odd, painful death.

Vaul said, "I've got five guys willing to go in with some very high-tech equi—"

"Just me," John said. "I'm going alone."

"Nobody's going to be hurt or killed. We're prepared this time."

"That's what it wants you to think. For your sake, and for the sake of these ignorant soldiers, don't order them in. They will die. I swear this to you. I've been in there, been in contact with the creature in there. It wants me alive for some reason. You know this."

Vaul bowed his head and scratched an eyebrow. He then looked into John's eyes and smiled. "You sure you'll be okay in there by yourself?"

"I'll do my best. It's all I can do."

"Do you need any safety measures? Weapons?"

John burped out a chuckle. "I don't even know what weapon will work against what's inside, if there even is one. And no equipment, either. It will just slow me down."

Vaul nodded and turned. Raising his voice, he spoke to everyone in the clearing, "Okay, listen up everybody."

Everyone stopped what they were doing and turned to him.

"Change of plans. Mr. John Rollings is going inside on his own. We have reason to believe that it's unsafe for anyone other than him to investigate the heart of the house. He will, however, be going in with a small tracking device. This will let us know where he is at any given moment, and how he's doing. Until he comes out, I don't want anybody within a hundred yards of the house. Is that clear?"

They looked at one another. Only a ballsy young soldier objected: "Sir, wouldn't that be more dangerous? For him, I mean?"

Vaul shot the kid a look. "I said, *is that clear?*"

The kid exhaled and nodded. "Yes, sir."

"Mr. Rollings has been inside more times than anyone

ever has. He knows the house better than anyone here. He has some sort of connection with that the thing inside. John is the only person to come out alive with his sanity intact." Vaul motioned to a large camouflaged tent, under which two young female soldiers were adjusting circuitry on a videocassette-shaped tracking device. John followed Vaul over to them, passed some crates marked FRAGILE, and stepped into the shade.

"These ladies will attach a sensor to your hand. It'll tell us many things after you're in," Vaul said. "Your body temperature and heartbeat, as well as information about your surroundings. It's got a tiny, impenetrable microphone, an even smaller camera that can record footage a full three-hundred and sixty degrees—much like the way a fly sees—and even a proctum sensor that can pick up traces of certain odors or gaseous elements that may be present in the air. Now, I know you don't want to go in with this, but I urge you to. Even if you don't come out, we can still examine the readings in the sensor remotely."

"That's encouraging, but last time your equipment took a shit." John laughed as the more attractive of the two women attached the warm, weightless contraption around his forearm. She stared into his eyes the whole time she secured the straps. He did the same, but as he peered into those lovely eyes, all he could think about was Jennifer, how much he missed her company, and how frustrating it was that she was married. Why are the good ones always taken?

She turned and walked away before he could entertain the thought any further.

"Okay." Vaul smiled and patted John on the shoulder. "It's your time now."

John held up his right arm, examining the sophisticated piece of equipment resting comfortably on his forearm. It looked like something out of a science fiction movie, with blinking red lights and triangular-shaped buttons with tiny holes under them.

"It's called a *Silicoter*. Don't tell anyone about it. It's supposed to be secret."

"I bet this would sell like crazy on Ebay," John joked.

"Don't get any ideas. And here. From the tests we've done, we know these UV lights will give plenty of needed illumination for you to see inside." Vaul handed him a long, narrow stick through which many tiny filaments could be seen. "Just click that button to turn it on. Are you ready to do this?"

John let out a deep breath. "I guess."

"Look at it this way, John. The sooner you do this, the sooner it will all be over with. Good luck." Vaul turned and looked up at the house as John walked toward it. John's palms were sweating, his mind racing. He could feel the sensor on his forearm vibrating very faintly against his skin. Vaul, Charlie, and all the others watched the door creak closed by itself once he was inside.

Dead bugs lay on their backs on the floor in the living room and in the kitchen, their little legs sticking up like tiny needles. John walked forward, toward the kitchen, unable to shake the idea that he needed to be upstairs, not below, to find the information he needed. He had been upstairs twice now, but maybe D'kourikai had purposely lured him away from the basement thus far to divert him from the truth.

There was nothing diverting him today, so John soon came to the basement door, opened it, and descended the steps slowly, one by one. Once his feet met with the concrete slab at the bottom, he raised a UV light high over his head. Though he got no weird vibes, there were blue ivy vines growing all over the ceiling. They did not look like any plantlike organism with which he was familiar. A mass connection of roots spawned every corner and rafter of the entire cellar. Attached to each long string were lightning-colored buds surrounded by small, slick whiskers.

John reached up with his free hand and felt the vine, then the bud, then the whiskers. Cold and wet and tingly. Upon further inspection, he noticed that the micro-thin whiskers were actually some kind of metal. Secondly, he noticed the odor. It reminded him of the pizza his grandmother used to make from scratch. A pungent, assaulting smell: *garlic.*

CHAPTER FOURTEEN

Just as John started his venture into the basement, Jennifer, standing back behind a tree twenty feet from the rear of the house, waited anxiously for two camo-clad gentlemen to go back around to the clearing so they wouldn't catch her snooping around. Her patience was quickly running thin. She stood quietly, still, her head peeking around a knot of an oak tree, her eyes focused on two acne-faced young men lugging around something that looked like a homemade microwave. They carried the heavy object back around the side of the house, their chubby forms almost out of sight. The young woman behind the tree made a dash for the back door. Sensing a spy, one of the two soldiers looked back, just missing spotting the outsider who had no business being here.

They continued lugging the box around to the front.

The woman opened the back door and entered. Her eyes adjusted to the difference in brightness. She could see very little, just small glimpses of retracted sunlight glimmering through the dusty window. After she closed the door behind her, she entered the pantry. The basement door ahead was cracked barely open. Through it, she could see the distinct luminescence of an ultraviolet light shining coolly within.

The basement's where stuff like this happens...she

remembered saying to John just yesterday.

She could wait no longer to see the house for herself. The energy she felt coming from the house was unmatched, unequaled, godly in a sense of raw power. The ripped wallpaper, the peeled paint, and the busted floors had layers beneath them, and layers farther beneath that. The house was the ultimate Ouija Board, open to all and bound by nothing.

Jennifer closed her eyes and took a few deep breaths, concentrating. She felt many things, many presences, many forms of energy. There was really no limit to the number of worlds floating through her mind...until she was disturbed from her trance when she heard a little girl *giggle*.

Jennifer opened her eyes. A small humanoid figure ran out of the basement and into the kitchen, out of her field of vision. There one second, gone the next.

"Hello?" Jennifer walked forward, through the pantry and into the kitchen. Once there, she saw no little girl; just a broken kitchen table and a very unsanitary-looking sink. Noticing a light switch out of the corner of her eye, she flicked it on.

Nothing.

The sound of a child giggling entered her ears again. Footsteps followed. They sounded close and low, then far and high.

Upstairs.

She followed the sound through the living room, then up the creaky wooden steps. All available light grew bleaker as she peaked at the curved banister top.

"Hello? I promise I'm not here to hurt you."

There was a faint thudding right overhead. She tilted her head back and looked up. The ceiling, though rotted and black all over, appeared distorted and uneven. It looked like there was a large rectangle etched into a small portion of it. Upon further examination, Jennifer noticed a small finger loop near one top of the rectangle.

Standing on her tip-toes, she reached for it. Grabbed it. Pulled it.

Boom!

It *opened up* with a large crash.

A staircase fell out along with a cloud of dust, leading the way to an attic. Carefully, cautiously, Jennifer climbed up into it, into the cleanest, most brightly-lit room she had been in thus far. The floor was unusually smooth, its surface coated with a thin layer of sawdust, whose scent lingered heavily in the air. The arched roof hanging over her shoulders was so sharp it made the height of the room disproportionally small to the floor. Regardless, this room seemed brand new, as if recently built by expert carpenters with immaculate skill. A huge beam of afternoon sunshine blazed through the window against the farthest wall, its warmth and radiance illuminating a little girl sitting on the floor, coloring on a sheet of paper.

She could not have been older than five or six, dressed in a bleached-white late-eighteenth or early-nineteenth-century dress, her hair fixed not unlike women from the Revolutionary Era. She had soft features, an upturned little nose, beautiful ice-blue eyes, and rosy-red cheeks stretched to form the smile of a young angel. The girl obviously wasn't from this time period, or even *alive*. Jennifer knew she was seeing a spirit in bodily form, following a routine *she* probably performed daily whilst stuck between worlds.

"Hi!" The girl's voice was sweet and buttery.

Jennifer paused. "Hello, honey." She walked over to her and knelt down. "What is your name?" Jennifer's voice was untidy and forced.

"Sandra. What's yours?" She did not look up from the drawing.

"I'm Jennifer. It's nice to meet you, Sandra."

Sandra looked up at her and grinned with all her teeth. "Did you come to save us?"

Jennifer didn't know how to respond to that question.

"We've been here a loooooong time."

"How did you get here, Sandra? Why are you here?"

"My Mommy and Daddy love me very much, that's why It'll kill me if I leave."

"It'll what?!"

"Shh. *It* might hear us."

"It's okay, Sandra. I won't let anything happen to you."

The little girl colored faster, harsher. "It doesn't want us to leave. It wants to feed on us."

"It?"

"I don't want to say its name. I don't like saying it. It comes when I say it."

Jennifer let out a deep breath. She couldn't believe she was talking to someone from the other side, someone who looked as tangible as herself.

"Sweetie, you can go into the light anytime."

"No! Light is bad. It gets us punished. Every time I get close to it, I get hurt. So does Mommy and Daddy. And the *other* lady."

"Punished? How? Who punishes you?"

The girl looked into Jennifer's eyes and put a finger against her own lips. "Shhhh. I think I hear It coming."

Jennifer looked around. Saw nobody. "It's okay. Trust me."

"No. Nothing's *ever* okay! Only pure life can destroy true death."

Jennifer glanced down at the picture the girl was drawing on an ancient, yellow piece of paper. It was an image of a small, silver pyramid suspended in the air and wrapped around a set of unfamiliar equations.

"What is this? What are you drawing?"

"The key. But the portal is—"

An explosion behind her caused her to quickly turned and lock her eyes on the attic door. It had slammed shut with tremendous force.

"Sandra, what—"

But when Jennifer turned to look at the little girl, she was gone. The piece of paper still lay on the floor, the crayon colors of the drawing bright under the intense sunlight. She picked it up and put it in her back pocket as she stood.

"Hear—me—go—out—th—" the little girl's faint and broken voice beckoned from some other world, both near and far. Jennifer looked around the room, searching for a presence. None was to be found.

Then she heard Sandra's voice again, loud and clear: *"Ruuuuun!"*

***

John shined the UV light around the basement, tracking the vines along the rafters toward the main source. As he went, he noticed changes in the color and shape of the ivy until it didn't even look plantlike anymore.

Before he knew it, a soft, rubbery mass wrapped itself around his leg. The light flew out of his hand. His face cracked off the cement basement floor.

Lying on his stomach, dazed, but still aware, he lifted his head and saw an immense, semi-mobile vegetation constructed of innumerable tendrils, leaves, and wooden branches all nestled together in a cocoon. Its very long, tentacle-like limbs, scarred with insect-sized holes, moved with jerky movements that also seemed a bit sluggish. The massive thing was thinner in the middle than it was at the top and bottom. The base was not connected to the ground. Small buds positioned in a variety of places popped open, revealing small, brightly-colored bulbs. These moved around like giant eyes. Every one of them sensed him. The stench of garlic increased exponentially, which, he figured, was the natural odor of this bizarre herb he hoped was not carnivorous.

He lay still, quiet, his breaths consciously slow. His eyes didn't sway from the monstrosity. *You don't see me. You don't see me. You don't see me.*

Slowly, its vine released his foot and slid away, the thorns attached to it trembling and squealing silently. It was almost back in the corner, out of harm's way, when John noticed a large ax resting against the wall seven feet to his left. Should he make a move for it? Use it to fend off the tentacle? Then make a run upstairs? Or make a run without going for the weapon?

John jumped to his feet, his right foot almost slipping in his own blood, and went for the ax. He only managed to take one step before the plant creature detected movement. Its leaves opened up to reveal thermal suckers underneath.

The longest tentacle flew across the room. John took another step, reaching for the wooden ax handle. He could see the tip of the plant's advancing appendage from the corner of his eye. It was halfway toward him already. Another one followed closely behind.

He took three more steps and lunged for the ax. His outstretched fingers touched, then knocked over, his only weapon. The tentacle passed right over his back. It just missed wrapping around his neck. The second oncoming tentacle changed trajectory, hitting and breaking the UV light, darkening the entire basement. John could see nothing. He now had to rely on instinct, sound, feel, and a little luck.

The plant had an unfair advantage. Its bulbed eyes could see heat through the darkness; it had more limbs, could reach far, and was faster.

John didn't stand a chance.

He lay still on the ground, his own blood filling the corners of his closed eyes. He could hear that the tendrils were close, moving near his face. His hands moved slowly, delicately, along the floor, searching for any type of weapon. His fingers brushed against a long, hard handle. *The ax!* He couldn't believe his luck!

As quietly as he could, he grabbed the weapon, slipped the base of the handle across his body, a mere millimeter or two beneath the vibrating tendril, and put it in position to strike with deadly power.

Sensing movement from below, a smaller part of the conscious ivy unwrapped itself from the larger part and poked at the soft, warm, pliable skin of the missing life-form. Both tendrils jerked back forcefully. A tiny shaft of light shining through the only window in the room lit up the head filled with silver, thorny teeth.

It shrieked, its voice like metal against metal, its leaves expanding from its main appendage, about to bite. John jerked upright and swung the ax. The blade swiped the tendril across the opening of its mouth, knocking off a couple of leaves and cutting out a couple thorns. It pulled away from all available light, thin green blood spurting from its sudden wound. This gave John enough time to stand and gain his balance. He swung the weapon sideways on instinct, unable to see if what he was swinging at was even in target range.

Immediately, he thought he'd made a gross mistake, until he felt the ax head catch, drag, and slice into the smaller tentacle against the sturdy brick wall. A liquid that smelled strongly of garlic hit him in his face. A sharp, agonized squeal filled the entire basement. The tentacles swung around in the darkness, back toward its main body. John turned and ran up the stairs, through the kitchen and living room. He could hear voices mumbling from above and went up to the second floor. The voices seemed to still be above him. He looked along the ceiling and saw where a door in the ceiling appeared to be welded shut.

The voice was so familiar. *Jennifer! How did she get in here?*

He barely finished the thought when the hatch door exploded in a flurry of splinters and chunks of metal. A staircase dropped out, along with a dark voice that said, "Enter, John." "

D'kourikai.

John's heart beat faster. The hairs on the back of his neck stood toward the ceiling.

The sooner you do this, the sooner you will get this over with.

Taking a deep breath, and acknowledging *what* he was about to face, he hiked up the thin wooden steps and entered the attic. Once he was inside, there was a loud thud. A new door, taking the place of the old one, sealed him in.

He wasn't going anywhere.

"Rooooollings...."

John looked across the room. D'kourikai was hanging upside-down from the ceiling, holding Jennifer's quivering body by her hair with its three webbed fingers. She cried quietly, unable to move, her face blank with horror. The crayon drawing was still gripped firmly in her right hand.

"So, we meet again, intuitive one." Orange slime oozed from its twisted form and onto the floorboards, onto the woman's shoulders, and against the walls, traveling in impossible directions at once. "Or should I say *both* intuitive ones? Or intuitive twos? A joke, of course." D'kourikai looked down at its female prey and sniffed her. As it did, the tears flowing down her cheeks were sucked into its flesh. "Ahh! The taste of emotion. Fear is your race's most primitive one. You have not yet learned how to conquer it...or merely *deal* with it. It's a waste of space. This female specimen is like you, John. I can tell you secrets about her she doesn't want you to know. She fears pain, love, and...flying? Your race can fly? Well, how did your kind figure that one out?"

John glanced around at its many eyes. They had no pupils, no identifiable emotion, nothing but nothing.

"Let her go," John demanded.

D'kourikai held her out. She whimpered.

"You want this weakling? Why should I give her to you? I like learning from her. I can absorb information by touch, y'know, just like you absorb information by reading—"

John took a step forward. D'kourikai held her farther out. The floorboards beneath her dangling feet rumbled, cracked, and snapped apart. The floor itself split open. Steam effused from the breach. She looked down as the wood fell away, under itself, into an abyss of black fire thousands of feet below. Jennifer looked like a piñata dangling over a volcano.

"Shall I drop her, John? Do you want to know what happens to physical bodies in these particular flames?"

John stepped back and held up his hands. "Okay, okay. Please, don't hurt her. If you want to take anyone, take me."

"When the time is right, I shall. You don't know it yet, but your race is already doomed. You were doomed to fail before you even began."

John swallowed. "What do you want?"

The entity laughed. Its entire form twitched in slow motion, normal motion, and then fast motion, as if unbound by speed. The falling slime followed in suit. Jennifer tried to keep from looking down, where the unbelievable colorless flames were burning dark.

"You already know what I want, John. This fallible waste—" D'kourikai shook Jennifer, "—tricked me into losing my connection to you. I want the barricade gone, or else I will drop her. Remove the object from your body and I will release her."

"And how will I know you'll live up to the bargain?"

"My dependable word, of course." It laughed viciously.

"And how do I know your word is dependable?"

"Do it now!"

John looked into Jennifer's lost eyes. The skin around them was red from crying. Tears rolled down her cheeks. To his surprise, she shook her head and mouthed the word *no*.

Don't take the wolfsbane out of your pocket.

He mouthed the word *sorry*, reached into his side pocket, and felt for the leaf. D'kourikai watched him with two smiles engraved on its wretched face. Jennifer fought futilely to protest. John's nervous fingers delved deep into the jean cavity. He felt lint, the wolfsbane, a piece of paper, and—a pill bottle?

The orange juice!

There was now a small crack in the bottom of the plastic container. Some of the O.J. had spilled out onto the pocket's other contents. He could already smell the sweet aroma of liquefied oranges.

"That's iiiiit!" D'kourikai was growing impatient. Its voice only got worse every time it spoke.

John removed the purple leaf from his pocket and held it up, his hand now sticky. He couldn't help but look at Jennifer, who tried to speak but was unable to.

"You'll let her go now."

"Release the safeguard first. Cast it four feet from your perimeter. I'll make it come to me. Then you will have your female friend."

John did just that. He tossed the wolfsbane forward. It froze in midair, glided slowly across the room, below a central rafter, over the blazing moat, and right into the beast's hand. Upon physical contact with the sacred wolfsbane, D'kourikai reacted violently.

The entity whined sharply, recoiled, and immediately dropped the leaf as if it were poison. Smoke effused from its burnt hand. John looked at Jennifer, who looked bewildered. She could not believe such a small, mediocre petal could do such harm to such a threatening antagonist. John, however, knew the wolfsbane had nothing to do with it.

Orange juice to the rescue!

The monster examined its wound, every one of its twenty-two eyes widening in unison. While it reacted to the pain of its injury, John shoved his hand into his pocket and yanked out the pill bottle. Using his index and thumb, he unfastened the cap, popped it off, and flung the entire container—along with its contents—at the monster.

I hope this works.

Jennifer watched as the improvised weapon flew in her direction, wondering just what John had concealed inside it. *Holy Water? Saltwater? Acid?* It made it over the separation in the middle of the floor, twirling, some of the liquid spilling out. John's arm was still extended as the object advanced speedily...then *slowly.* D'kourikai looked up from its wounded hand to see it closing in. With one crazed look, he made the bottle stop in mid-air, only one foot away from his twisted face. *"You bastard of Earth. Try to hurt meeeee!"*

Jennifer could smell the oranges. Giving the creature a crazed look of her own, she bravely reached out and knocked the juice all over its head.

John cringed. Jennifer momentarily went deaf. The

monster let go of her hair and grabbed its steaming, melting face in agony. She fell downward, between the cracks in the floor, flailing her arms. John ran forward and dove, reaching out. His body slid across the sawdust-covered floor. He watched her disappear from view and into the chasm of certifiable death. Black light billowed out. A female human scream sounded, but it was not nearly as loud as the one from D'kourikai.

With his arm fully extended, and his whole frame going a little too fast, John plunged his hand into the trench, stretching to grab onto Jennifer. He felt nothing...nothing...and then something. His fingers coiled around a soft mass of skin and bone. He had grasped hold of her wrist.

Her bodyweight pulled him over the cliff's edge. He could see down into the pit of destruction, could see boiling, black lava bubbling and releasing pillows of red gas. Things swam in the heat, things too far away to be distinguishable by human eyes. The scene looked like a color-inverted, Catholic version of Hell.

"I got you!"

"Don't let go! Pull me up, John!"

His arm trembling, he pulled. The veins protruding from his forehead looked like they were going to rupture. Sweat puddled off his face and onto hers. She held on for dear life.

"Hold on, Jennifer!" He looked into her eyes. *"I got you. Trust me."* He assured her with a smile, got his bearings, and pulled again, this time with both hands. Every muscle in his upper body vibrated and ached, but his efforts weren't paying off.

"Come on! You have to help me. Climb!"

D'kourikai's face smoldered as its cries began to die off. Its head wobbling, it spewed acidic saliva from its bulging mouth. Some of the fluid sprayed dangerously close to Jennifer's back.

She propped her feet on an outcropping of wood protruding from the wall, and pushed. Her calves burned. Her feet trembled. John resituated himself. His palms were so sweaty, he was losing his grip. It was like trying to tug an octopus by its greasy tentacle. Besides that, he was not in the right position. He needed to be standing with his feet under him, not lying on his stomach.

"Jennifer!"

"John! Don't let me go!"

He couldn't help it. He did. Her hands slid out of his. She began to fall. John felt his stomach fall with her. He thought she was a goner. *I can't save anybody.*

But she only ended up falling three feet before landing on a board that miraculously broke her fall.

Jennifer stumbled, her hands still skyward, where John grabbed them. He was now standing, with a look of resolution on his face. He yanked her out of the hole with ease.

They ran to the staircase, which was now open. Jennifer darted down, but John looked back at D'kourikai, who was now shaking off its injury.

Standing near It, dressed in early-nineteenth century clothing, was the apparition of an adult male figure who looked familiar to John.

It was the ghost of Charles Prestillion, the builder of this house.

He looked sad, tormented, and peaceful all at once. He nodded as John left the attic, as if thanking him.

Both out of the attic, John and Jennifer ran down the main set of steps and out through the front door into the clearing where some fifty soldiers were waiting for them.

***

Vaul watched them retreat toward the road, wondering who the woman was and how she'd gotten here. Meanwhile, a young, bald soldier standing by the porch walked up to the door and peeked inside the dreadful house, in awe. Another nearby soldier, a small-chested woman with a big nose, saw him getting too close. Her mouth dropped open and a scream came out: *"Jimmy!!!"*

Vaul swung his head back to the house, eyebrows raised. *"Geeeeeet awaaaaaay from there, you fools!"*

It was as if a bomb had gone off. The young bald gentleman peeking inside the doorway was sucked into the dark house like an ant into a vacuum cleaner. He didn't even have the chance to grunt. However, another noise resonated loudly.

Spissssssh!

Every window of the house exploded at the same time. Glass scattered, showering everyone in the vicinity of the clearing with deadly shrapnel. Some people covered themselves; others turned away or ran. Those unfortunate enough to catch the full brunt of the blast were chopped to pieces, filling the clearing with mud of bloody dirt, and littering it with scattered limbs.

John and Jennifer had managed to find cover behind a wide tree near the northernmost corner of the clearing, and looked around it to see what was going on.

Every piece of descending shrapnel inexplicably continued to float through the air with what appeared to be some form of manipulation, as if they were being control by some force. Sparkling bits of glass hovered, almost motionless, only feet away. One soldier, who had survived the initial blast by hiding behind a thick bush, stood and reached out to grab a piece of the suspended glass. As his fingers enclosed around the shard, it began spinning, slicing off every finger on that hand. The soldier turned away from the house and began running. Three pieces of glass gave chase and embedded themselves in his spine, killing him instantly.

John knew D'kourukai was responsible.

As if to confirm this hypothesis, an immensely powerful voice blasted through the opening of every broken window. *"Rooooooollings!"*

"Oh shit," John muttered.

Not one breath could have been drawn before a bigger catastrophe occurred. The suspended fragments of glass were set into motion again, this time as fast as high-speed bullets. Several people were hit by the debris and killed instantly. Those that were not hit, or were only maimed, were airborne themselves.

A strong, hurricane-force wind suddenly blew through the clearing, knocking people off their feet and lifting them skyward. John and Jennifer were the first to grab onto the branches of a tree for support. Grass was ripped from the ground. Expensive military computer equipment fell off tables and smashed together as they flew upward. People reached for land way after their bodies were yanked out of their shoes and toward the house. Many were sucked in through the broken windows. Some slammed fatally against the monstrosity before entry.

Vaul fell and slid across a patch of mud, bumping into a scared young soldier clutching onto a tree root. The boy couldn't have been any older than twenty, his eyes filled with tears, his rationality completely gone. His face was bleeding profusely from where small particles of glass had struck. Drool oozed from his bottom lip. The root he was clinging to looked strong and deep.

"Momma! Momma!" he screamed, looking around blankly, his eyes glazing over. Flying twigs pummeled his

face, drawing extra tears. His clothes fluttered harshly.

Vaul broke eye-contact with him when his own two-hundred-pound frame began to skid farther across the clearing. In a panic, he plunged his fingertips into a mound of dirt, gripping onto quickly-crumbling soil. He scanned the immediate area for something stronger, and noticed the young soldier's feet quivering only a few yards away. Hopefully, if he grabbed onto a boot, and that boy's grip was firm enough, he could ride this out.

He crawled toward it, using the ground as a sturdy counterpart.

One unfortunate victim bounced off dry land, went violently into the air toward the uppermost window, missed it completely, and slammed against the house so hard he died upon impact. His limp body flew over the roof and was subsequently sucked down in through the chimney. Another man, trying to outrun the mayhem, stopped mid-stride; the suction yanked him backward with brute force, where his back collided horribly with the edge of the porch roof. The growing force of the wind immediately ripped his arms and legs apart. His right arm and leg went in through the right window, and his left arm and leg, the left. His torso went in through the doorway; blood splattered everywhere.

John and Jennifer, their lower bodies now hanging in the air, remained clinging onto two crisscrossed tree limbs. Her long hair blew every which way.

John looked toward the outside entrance of the woods that bordered the path to the house. His eyes focused in on a chewed point in the grass where the ground was undisturbed by the raging winds, where nothing on the ground was moving at all, possibly the boundary point of D'kourikai's control.

Maybe his sight and power cannot penetrate as far as I

thought. Only with my DNA can he extend his sight. Three feet prior to the military barricade. That's it!

A bulky computer system crashed into a porch column, where it obliterated into pieces. A dying shrub went into a lower-story window, while another lifeless body *bashed* against an upper-story window frame before flying in through it.

Down in the clearing, hardly anybody was left. John and Jennifer were still dangling from a tree; two male soldiers were clinging to the bumper of a small Jeep; one young, injured female had a firm hold of an outcropping of a rock; and Vaul was still struggling to reach the soldier's foot.

Just when he grabbed it, the kid panicked and kicked him in the face, cutting his lip wide open.

Still, he continued forward. Grabbed it again. Again, the kid booted him, harder this time. Blood run from Vaul's nose and trailed across his face.

"Asshole! Help me!"

The soldier didn't look back, didn't hear him, or just didn't care.

Vaul could hold onto earth no longer. He needed something more tangible.

Clenching his teeth, he reached out and grabbed the kid's boot once more. The young soldier cocked his leg back and power-heeled him. *Hard.* His body turned to jelly. The scale-force winds picked him up and back toward the house.

And then, without warning, all commotion and chaos ceased, the glass dropping to the ground, and the wind coming to a stand-still.

Vaul, miraculously, landed safely by the house's foundation, shaken but all right, just as John and Jennifer dropped into the grass.

A peaceful cloak of silence enveloped the clearing. Every

remaining survivor sat or lay still, none able to accept it all—or any of it, for that matter. It was too incredible to be real, too chaotic an experience for the ordinary mind to process. The soldier who'd booted Vaul in the face was the only one making noise, crying. Jen looked over at John, who returned the look.

She was the first to speak. "Maybe you were right. Maybe I should have waited before coming out here."

John laughed. He didn't mean to, but it just came out.

Vaul examined his surroundings and his remaining men. Only four were accounted for out of more than fifty, the house having swallowed the majority of them.

The two soldiers by the Jeep loosened their grip on the bumper but didn't actually let it go just in case complete pandemonium broke out again. One man was in shock; the other, a stubborn, hard-headed veteran, looked energized. The girl lying close to Vaul let go of the rock and looked up at the house, unable to believe the windows were once again in their original places, without so much as a scratch on them. Twenty yards away from her, the hysteric, disturbed boy still clutching onto a tree root stopped calling for his momma and began to chant a new phrase over and over again.

"Rock a bye Rollings. Your time is near. Your soul will be going, *and mine will be soon here! Everywhere!*"

CHAPTER FIFTEEN

Jennifer's Blazer screeched around a descending curve on Robin's Pike, sending rocks flying up from the rear tires.

"I thought I knew what I was getting into. I guess I was mistaken." She struggled to hold onto the wheel with her trembling hands. John sat in the passenger seat beside her, not near as tense. They were both headed back to her new stay.

"It's okay. Memorable though, wasn't it?"

"Memorable?" She held back a chuckle. "You know how many nightmares I'm going to have for the next four years? Night terrors, not just nightmares. That was insane!"

Within minutes, Jennifer flicked the turn signal again and turned into her driveway and parked behind a black Sedan. After placing the gear in park, she gestured to the small, white house on the right. "Here's my place. Well, my new place."

John got out and looked at the vinyl-sided bungalow. It was trailer-shaped, had recently been painted, the porch grossly decorated with wicker crafts corresponding to Native American symbolism. The entire perimeter was enclosed by one tall, wrap-around chain-link fence. It served the purpose of keeping three dogs—and Lucky—from running off. Lucky was already sitting and waiting near a dilapidated dog house, tail wagging, excited to see John once again. The other dogs were barking up a storm somewhere behind the house.

"Lucky!" John reached over the fence to petted his best friend. The dog jumped up, set his front paws on his master's shoulders, and licked his face. "I missed you, pal. How have you been? How are you doing? Have they been treating you good here?"

Jennifer got out and shut her car door. A smile emerged on her face as she watched them reunite. This was exactly what she needed to see after enduring the most nightmarish experience of her life. "He's been whimpering around for you. I think he missed you more."

John scratched Lucky's side and patted him on the back. "Did you miss me? Did you miss me? You were whimpering for me, huh? You're such a good boy!"

**

The interior of the house smelled heavily of jasmine potpourri and looked spotless. The wood-laminated floors were still somewhat slick from an early-morning mopping. Dream catchers hung from every major window John could see in view; other objects of similar use and origin were set up on tables and stands or were hanging from hooks on walls. To the left was an open kitchen, where a small Maytag fridge rumbled quietly. Straight ahead stretched a long, narrow hall that led to bedrooms and a bathroom. To the right, through an arched doorway, was the living room: a small, carpeted space accompanying a wooden Indian and a large flat screen HDTV—the kind John always wished he had. Currently, the channel was tuned to Judge Judy, who was busy scolding a young, dumb-looking adolescent.

"Make yourself at home." Jennifer brushed past him and entered the kitchen. "You want something to drink? Got water, soda, even got beer, if you like. I suppose you're not in the mood for orange juice right now?" She chuckled.

"Soda's fine."

She grabbed two from the refrigerator. "What do you think did it?" She handed John a Pepsi. "That—*thing*—had a severe allergic reaction to orange juice. Vitamin C? Citric acid? What chemical do you think burned it like that?"

"I have no idea." Standing dumbly in the hallway, John watched the television.

"As I said, make yourself at home. I need to kick back for a while anyway." Jennifer opened the front door for a moment. "Come on, Lucky!"

Lucky flew inside, going straight to John's side.

"We usually don't let him inside, but it'll be all right just this once." Jennifer closed the door and entered the living room. John followed her in. She took a seat on a recliner; he sat on a small suede sofa.

"There was a time today when I thought I wouldn't come home again. God, I can't believe you're so mellow right now. What we've just been through—" Jennifer started.

John smiled and took a big drink of cola. "I assume I can trust you won't be going back?"

"You got that right! I will pray for you, your safety, but I can't go near there again. I know I said I would help, but—" Jennifer trailed off.

"Don't say any more. There's no need to explain."

Lucky knelt by John's feet and scratched at his pant leg. John patted him lightly on the head. "Hey there, buddy."

Jennifer cracked open her can of soda. Carbonated beverage foamed from the breach. She quickly used her mouth to soak it up before it spilled onto her lap.

"Hey, I'm heading out to work!" said a male voice.

Startled, John dropped his soda on the floor and turned immediately to see who it was. He expected to see twenty-two horrible eyes watching him. Instead, he saw the same man he had seen in the hospital the day after the United Apartments had burned down. John presumed to be Jennifer's husband. He was standing in the doorway now, dressed in a McDonald's work uniform, keys in hand, an apologetic look on his dark face. "Sorry, man, didn't mean to scare you."

John quickly picked up the can of Pepsi before soda poured out everywhere.

"It's okay." Jennifer waved for him to enter. "I don't think I've introduced you two yet. Harold, this is—"

"Can you introduce us later? I don't mean to be rude, but I'm waaaay late for work." The man pointed to his watch, turned, his black ponytail swaying from side to side as he hurried out the door.

John exchanged a look with Jennifer. She chuckled. "That's Harold, Mr. Personable. He can be so reticent at times. I tell you, he can be the most stubborn out of all my brothers."

"Your brother? I thought he was your—"

Jennifer smacked her knee and laughed. "You thought we were married? Dating? Oh hell nooooo." She laughed. "We're siblings. You couldn't tell we had the same facial features? Same hooked nose? Same lips? No, he's one of my brothers. He's the only one of my siblings who isn't married. And he was more than willing to take me."

John looked around the room, as if searching. "Where is your other half then? I don't think I've seen him before." He wanted to shout *I'm in love with you, Jennifer!*

"He's been...out of town for a while. On business, y'know. He has to fly around a lot, and me, I am more grounded than he is. I'm not much of a traveler. Never was." She nervously twisted the wedding band on her finger. A look of sadness flourished in her eyes. It was obvious she did not want to discuss this any further, as if it pained her to talk about the mystery man she was married to. What was she hiding?

He changed the subject. "I found one thing out about the house."

She looked at him. Some of her visible sadness was gone. "What?"

"There's a border that surrounds it. Where it stops, D'kourikai cannot see past unless given certain rights to cross it."

"Like the lock of your hair."

"Yes, a key, in a sense."

"Key...key," Jennifer remembered something. "I almost forgot!" She reached into her back pocket and pulled something out: the folded piece of paper Sandra had given her back in the attic. "She gave this to me and said something about a key, a portal." Jennifer got out of her chair, sat beside John, and unfolded the old, dusty sheet of paper, revealing the crayon drawing of the silver pyramid within.

"It *has* to have a connection with the source of it all," Jennifer offered.

"I think that plant creature in the basement might be guarding something important. This could be it."

"John, I didn't tell you about the girl I saw. She was about nine-years-old, dressed for the early eighteenth century, who gave me this and said...Jesus, what did she say?" Jennifer thought about it long and hard. "Before D'kourikai appeared, the girl said to me... *this is the key, but the portal is—*' and then she trailed off."

"Sandra Prestillion, you mean?"

"Sandra!" Jennifer's eyes lit up. "Yes, that's what she said her name was."

"Sandra was the daughter of the man who built the house back in the seventeen-hundreds. I think I saw him before I left the attic. I got a feeling from him that *he* had something to do with the ledge you landed on when you...fell.''

Jennifer pointed to some of the equations written on the paper. "And what do you suppose these are? Doesn't look like any math I've ever learned in school.''

"Looks Greek to me. Either way, somebody's trying to tell us something with this.''

"There's more.'' Jennifer looked into John's eyes, then looked away, as if uncomfortable. "Sandra distinctly said *'only pure life can destroy true death.'* She also said that D'kourikai was keeping her, her mom, her dad, and some woman, like slaves. Does this mean anything?''

John stared ahead, the drawing clutched tightly in his hands. "Only pure life can destroy true death? Could mean a few different things. Pure life can be looked at as a newborn just coming into the world. This, some say, can override certain forms of death.''

"Couldn't the reference 'pure life' mean a human made in the image of God, and 'true death' mean the thing that's in control of that house? Good versus evil?''

John smiled. "Yes, you could be right.''

"What do you suggest we do then?''

"I don't know. First, we need to find out what these equations mean. Then we need to figure out—'' John absentmindedly turned the paper over, revealing a whole new page of information neither he nor Jennifer expected to see. On the reverse side was one small disorganized paragraph of words written in a hurried script: *Savior, look down, look up. Feel up, fall down. Jarsky wasn't (blotched word) Jarsky and greatest (more blotched out words) Answer is within the (blotched word) It wasn't meant to go this route. Hell has been unleashed. It will spread (blotched word) unless confined. Nothing more I, nor (many blotched words)....*

The Jarsky pro-(blotch) was (blotch) staple in the new development of— (a huge blank space)....

John's eyes quickly zoned in on the bottom of the page and on the last few visible words and digits he could make out. It was an address, circled and underlined.

2219 Caroni Street, Bellsville, PA.

"What does it mean?" Jennifer could barely contain her curiosity. Her increasingly squeaky voice revealed this fact. "Do you understand any of it? Most of it seems incoherent!"

"Incoherent? I don't think it's meant to be; I think it was hurried before the entirety of this clue was completely destroyed."

"By what?"

"D'kourikai," John sighed. "What else?"

"Are you familiar with that address?"

"I am."

"Well, where is that place?"

"It's where the abandoned Gerriton Warehouse used to be."

"What are we waiting for?" Jennifer jumped to her feet. "Let's go!"

"Okay."

***

Jennifer's Blazer pulled into a faded parking space behind an old, abandoned brick building standing on the banks of the Ohio River. The driver's and passenger's side doors opened simultaneously. Jennifer and John stepped out into a cold, strong passing gust.

He saw a line of school buses headed toward Steubenville across the river. He closed his eyes and took a deep breath.

"John, you coming? What are you doing?"

He smiled, almost laughed. "Nothing. I'm doing nothing. It's the best thing in the world to do. Nothing can compare to it."

"Nothing can compare to nothing, huh?" Jennifer joked.

John gazed at the river for one last second. "Yeah, it's like dividing by zero. Let's figure out once and for all what we're dealing with. I'm already sick of this entity. Even though he can no longer trace me, I still feel him close, searching."

"There's a window over there already broken. It's pretty small, but I think we can squeeze through."

Jennifer and John walked over to the corner of the three-story building, near a gutted old walkway, to a shattered basement window. Dirty glass littered the sill, the ground, and the ledge within. The opening, though not huge, was wide enough to crawl through with some effort.

John thoroughly kicked as much of the broken shards out of the way, clearing a path. Afterward, he looked at Jennifer, who was kneeling but not entering.

"What? You want *me* to go in first?" She laughed in disbelief.

John offered a joke of his own. "You know what they say. Ladies first."

"Well, thanks, John, but I really insist you go ahead."

John knelt down, planted his butt on the moldy ground, and snaked his way feet-first in through the opening. Once inside, he offered Jennifer a hand. "You coming? Or would you rather me unlock and open a door for you?"

She gave her hand. He carefully helped her in through the gap, which was no higher than three feet and no wider than five. Her small frame slowly wiggled through, her back arching awkwardly, her free hand gripping the top of the windowsill. She almost fell once.

"I gotcha. Just watch the glass," John said, his body close to hers. He could smell her perfume, her breath. Her eyes were darker than he thought they were, and he could hear her steady breathing. Not once during his assisting her did she look at him. She even seemed uncomfortable that he was touching her at all.

John broke contact with her once her feet met with solid ground.

"Sorry." He took a step back, giving her space.

"No, it's okay. It's just—"

"Just what?" He thought he knew what the issue was. As his hands touched her body, a part of him lusted for touching all of her. Maybe she felt that. Maybe she wanted it too, but she was married.

She responded to his question, "I was just going to say watch where you put your hands. I'm a little skittish about physical contact." She then produced and handed him an unlit glow stick she'd found in the backseat of her Blazer. "Here." He took it and broke it open. The dark storeroom burned to life with red light. Jennifer broke open a green stick of her own.

"Looks like we picked the right room from the start," John muttered, his voice faint and distorted in the small room. They both held up their improvised flashlights to examine their surroundings. The place was in shambles, littered with old papers, boxes, crates, rows and rows of rusty file cabinets, a movable chalkboard with equations written on it, dusty desks with some strange diagrams scratched into the wood, and, in the far corner, miniature multicolored pyramids hanging from the ceiling to the floor by small metal wires.

"Where do we begin?" Jennifer felt overwhelmed with the tedious amount of data they would have to sort through. It showed in her face and in her tone of voice.

John panned around in one long motion. "You got that drawing?"

She slipped it into his hand without saying a word. He

looked at it and rushed over to the chalkboard. She followed closely behind.

With a sleeve, he lightly brushed away a layer of dust to reveal the writings beneath and read them aloud. "The Jarksy Experiment can be understood in laymen's terms as the complete collaboration of energy and matter. Space and time do not exist in the third dimension. They can be combined to connect to another *dimension* that exists around us everywhere, every time. There is only one geometric figure that provides the special key. This key is essential in opening the door to the path of light. This symbol has been used for many centuries in Egypt...*the pyramid*—a perfectly conformed combination of life and symmetry. This opens the *sphere*—a symbol of renewal and attachment. When these two elements fuse together, they create the greatest power known to man, an equation of utmost importance...."

John wiped away some more dust at the bottom of the board. Jennifer shined her glow stick over it.

"L/V^2?" She lowered her eyebrows. "I've seen this somewhere before. This equation."

"Like I said before, looks Greek to me."

"No, no, it's...I really have seen this before." She thought for a moment longer before it struck her. "Matter and energy conversion! That's it! Energy is equal to mass times the speed of light squared!"

"I'm no genius, but that's $E = mc^2$, not this equation."

"Not if Prestillion discovered the equation in the late-eighteenth or early-nineteenth century."

"Are you serious?"

"Yes. You know, maybe Prestillion was on to something here. The relationship between matter and energy...maybe—"

"Maybe it acts as a sort of key," John finished.

He rushed over to the three small pyramids in the far

corner of the room. Jennifer had to run to keep up with him. The reflections from the green and red glow sticks bounced off the walls like strobe lights.

"But how did he do it?" John approached the first—a blue pyramid hanging by two thin metal rods. "As far as I know, what he was able to do transcends even modern science."

For a long time, John and Jennifer examined the pyramid. Its sides were impossibly flat, and the edges and tips were sharp as razors. Its blue color was exquisite, bright, almost glowing, unlike any material either of the two had ever seen. It had been meticulously constructed, so much so that John thought it was geometrically flawless, down to the minutest unit of measurement.

Curious, he slowly reached out with his right hand and brought it close to the sacred object. The tip of his middle finger made contact with a side. The surface was smooth, somehow soft and substantially hard at the same time.

"John, do you feel anything?"

He didn't.

Then he *did.* It was very subtle at first, a gentle sensation of electricity flowing into his palm. Wanting more, he put his whole hand against the small pyramid, gripping it like a ball. The sensation intensified. It felt as if twenty volts of current were running up his arm, through his body, into his feet, around his brain. He had never felt anything like it.

But it wasn't until he touched the topmost point when something really amazing happened. A massive surge of energy coursed through him in a wave of tingling needles burning into much more than just his nerves. He could feel it in the core his bones, his cells, his hair follicles. It didn't hurt, was not the least bit painful. It was a pleasant sensation accompanied by a *wowwing* sound and a bright, blast of light.

He could sense life forms swarming around him—behind him, across the room, the river, the world—oblivious to him. He could not see them, but he was certain they were there and had always been there.

"John? John?" Jennifer tugged at his shirt. He had been catatonic for the last several seconds.

Finally, he broke contact and stepped away.

"What did you see? What happened?" She demanded to know.

"I saw the light—the sun, maybe—and..." his mind searched for a metaphor, "and I felt the hand of God."

A light flashed inside Jennifer's head. Her eyes lit up, as if she was onto something. "I watched this show on Discovery a while back, about stars. They burn through nuclear fusion. The pressure within a star fuses hydrogen nuclei together to form helium, but the atomic weight of the helium atom produced is less than the weight of the hydrogen used to construct it. Since matter and energy must be conserved..."

"...the missing mass must be converted to energy," John finished, understanding what Jennifer was saying. "And that's what powers stars."

"Right. Well, when the star runs out of hydrogen, it stars fusing helium into heavier elements, and those heavy elements into heavier elements, and so forth. I think when it gets to iron, the amount of energy produced is not sufficient to prevent the pressure from the star's gravity from causing it to collapse on itself—"

John nodded with a smile. "Causing an explosion and a sometimes a black hole. So is that what this could be about? Prestillion was trying to create a black hole? That's gotta be it! And the black hole is not just a singularity, but a portal to another world! That's why D'kourikai has power limited to the particular area. It's not fully open yet!"

"At least, not until the entity—"

"Needs me," he finished her sentence. "When all hell breaks loose. If we don't stop it, not only will it consume our world, it will consume every world it can."

"Wait, what about ghosts? The spirit world?"

John shook his head doubtfully. "I don't know. But I know that *It* knows about the spirit world somehow. It made an indirect reference to it that I didn't understand 'til later. However, if it can trap the disembodied Prestillion family, along with other beings, it may be able to trap and destroy pretty much anything."

Jennifer didn't look hopeful, but she stared at the triple pyramids the way a child does a brand new toy. She thought she could feel energy vibrating from the one closest to her, like the rim of a wine glass being stroked by a moist finger. She wanted to touch it so badly, the desire was almost overwhelming. John could see it in her eyes.

"Later. We will come back to it. Then you can see for yourself what really exists in the cracks between life." John went his own way, pushing past her, the luminosity of his glow stick growing gradually weaker. He seemed to be in a hurry, on a mission, not knowing where to go next. Some information had presented itself, but not enough to satisfy his appetite. There were so many scattered papers covering the floor, the desks, and the file cabinets, that it would have likely taken decades just to read them all.

A hand fell on his shoulder. He jumped, spun around.

"Easy, chief. It's just me." Jennifer offered him a comforting smile. "I found something. Listen to this. The Jarsky Project is an experiment that may be a breakthrough, even by today's standards. It calls for 'the disintegration of specially-designed atoms which are not naturally occurring but are man-made. This consists of a new gaseous element, void of carbon and infused with strong protonic particles and plasmic ions. Though it is technically gaseous, the properties of the substance act, look, and feel like liquid. It has enough energetic potential in one single gram to power a small country for weeks. It has many possible uses; however, it is exceedingly expensive to produce.'

"'We believe we can do the impossible: uncover a co-existing world wrapped within the interior of this one, a possible extra-dimensional plane of life where the threshold of physical matter cannot currently dwell. I believe we can open up a door to the spirit realm, a gateway to Heaven.'" Jennifer looked up at John, her mouth agape. "Heaven?"

"Hmm. Well," he shrugged his shoulders, "maybe that was his intention. The man who tried to cure headaches with Nitroglycerin blew himself up. He created the first real explosive. You shoot for the heavens, sometimes you end up in hell. Read on."

She did. "'Whether the experiment works or not, only time will tell. We are finalizing the design of the pyramid, which is the key, and the silver sphere, which is the door. Both are made from previously unknown, man-made metals, and both possess great strength and highly magnetic fields beyond the scope of anything ever tested. These, set vertically at the precise distance apart, via connection with this new element housed in tubing, should create a peculiar omni-directional force of intense energy thus far undiscovered by man.'" Jennifer stopped to catch her breath, and then turned the page.

"Vertically..." John rubbed his chin, thinking. "At the precise distance apart?" He took the drawing out of his pocket, opened it up, and read. "'Savior, look down, look up.' I think that is what he was trying to tell us. *We're* the saviors.

They're counting on us to save them."

Jennifer scratched her head. "As soon as I entered that house, I felt an uncanny and overwhelming sense that something vital was upstairs."

"As did I. We know that the key is downstairs."

"The attic...it looked completely opposite from the downstairs—even the upstairs hallway, for that matter. It was much cleaner and smelled like new."

"Look down, look up. The portal is open...in the *attic!*" John felt the puzzle pieces finally coming together. "The house is just the conductor."

"But why his house and not a laboratory?"

"'Cause his family died in that house! Something about poisoning."

"Before or after the Jarksy Project?" she pushed.

"It has to have been before. Why else would you even want to rip open a path to the spirit world? If your whole family died in a house that you built for them and you inadvertently killed them by building it over some underground pipeline, what would you do? Especially if you were a genius like Charles Prestillion?

"What if he *knew* his family was forever trapped inside that house as ghosts? As souls bound to Earth because they died before their real time? Maybe he couldn't live without them and wanted to see them and communicate with them again. Psychic energy like that doesn't just go away, it stays around forever. That's gotta be why he built it there and not here, in some warehouse."

"'*Feel* up, fall *down*', the paper says!" Jennifer's gross realization was evident in her excited voice. "Feel up would mean his connection to his family, to Heaven. Wanting to feel close to them again. Fall down would mean it didn't work—"

"That it came crashing down!" John nodded, red glow

stick light illuminating one half of his face, and green, the other. He looked otherworldly, himself.

"Now how do we stop it?"

Just as she finished saying this, a gentle, cool breeze blew in through the broken window, across the room, and passed between both investigators. It stirred papers, threw some around, and did the unexpected. It deliberately flipped through the pages of the manuscript cradled in Jennifer's hands, all the way to one of the last pages in the text.

John and Jennifer looked at each other and then down at the explanation under their very noses. The top of the page read: *Status: Failure*. Under that, everything was written by hand in inked text. John read it fast, nervously.

"'I only meant to unlock the boundaries between Earth and Heaven; instead, I have unleashed alternate levels of Hell—hellish worlds, anyway. There must have been hundreds I've seen in one swift glance. I now have feelings and urges impossible to describe. Human eyes have been concealed from multiple unknown truths since the beginning of time. Now I see why. Horrible things are around us and within us at all times. *Some of them can interact with us without our knowing it!* I had not foreseen this in the beginning and cannot end it anytime during my life. There are realms beyond Heaven, Earth, and Hell. There are life forms like us, and life forms I dare not mention, or else I could die. I will die soon. It told me I would. This thing named D'kourikai has my family. He collects their souls, collects many souls. Soon it will have mine. There's nothing I can do. I was so obsessed with reuniting with my deceased family that I'd overlooked every danger imaginable. I've opened Pandora's Box. All my colleagues were eaten and burned alive. They had no chance. The hole in the attic of my house is not white like I'd expected, it's *black*. Void of anything holy. The only thing I can do now is wait. D'kourikai can see me, has a hold of me wherever I go. Oh no...I feel him coming! He's closing in on me. I have to finish this. Fast! If anyone reads this, I just want to say I failed my mission of bringing Heaven to Earth. If this monstrous being is the ultimate embodiment of evil, then only one thing has the power to stop it. *Maybe*. Something I'm not. And that is the ultimate embodiment of good. Pure life. A *mystical* mortal with absolute s—'"

John slammed a fist down on the table. "Dammit!"

"What? Absolute what?"

"The 'S' is there, but that's it. After that, it's been marked out."

"Here, let me see." She quickly but carefully looked over the whole page, making note of the spaces between other words and the length and penmanship of each word. Her eyes went from left to right at blinding speed. "Whatever word it is, it's between nine and thirteen letters long. What could that be?"

"That single word could mean the difference between total disaster and closing the portal." John ran a hand nervously through his hair. A hint of anger burned in his eyes.

"When we get back, I'll go through a dictionary to see if I can find a word that could match," Jennifer said.

John nodded, relieved and stressed all at once. The glow sticks were beginning to fizzle out. The luminosity they produced now was barely brighter than two nightlights.

"Look for a word pertaining to a single person."

"What do you make of the reference to a mystical mortal?"

He shook his head. "I think mortal means embodied, as in alive, physically. I think mystical means...."

"John, I think it may be time you stop denying these

abilities you have. You *are* a mystic, a psychic," Jennifer said with a smile.

John looked at her, his eyes dormant and glassy.

"You're the weapon—you, John."

CHAPTER SIXTEEN

The ride back to Ben's was bumpy and boring. The houses John gazed at through the passenger-side window as they drove through Bellsville and toward Lecorrd flew by in an unseen blur. Red lights turned to green at every intersection, and STOP signs seemed to appear at every corner. John was getting sick of the stop-and-go routine, but at around six o' clock, right before dusk, the rumbling Blazer pulled up to the curb on Maynor Street after what seemed like two long hours. John got out. "Thanks for the ride back, Jen."

"I'll call you as soon as I figure out that word. Then we, or you, can defeat D'kourikai once and for all." She smiled. In this particular light, during this particular moment, at this particular location, her smile was perfect. "Take it easy."

He managed a grin and shut the door. The Jeep pulled away.

It was cold out, probably the coldest day so far this fall. No higher than thirty degrees. Tiny, sporadic flakes of snow fell from the sky very slowly. Smoke billowed from the furnaces and fireplaces of almost every nearby residence. The streets were vacant of human life, even working vehicles. Nobody around for miles wanted anything to do with this frigid weather.

John looked up at Ben's rundown house. The shutters were dangling, the gutters broken. Quite a few shingles were missing from the roof. It looked unoccupied, though an upstairs light was on. He knew his friend was home, and unexpectedly *felt* that his friend was close to a different home, one unexplored by physical eyes. A home only offered to bodiless life forms.

Oh no. Not now. Not today.

A feeling of despair pervaded him as he stood there looking up at the room his friend was rotting in, probably dying in. His heart ached. He did not want to face him but knew he must.

He walked up onto the porch, into the house, and into the unoccupied living room, where the television was blaring. The local news was on, and Dana Richardson, a beautiful Latina who always wore a tight, silky, breast-accentuating blouse, was reporting. Her lips moved fast. Her voice resounded slightly slower. She was talking about an issue John did not want to hear—cancer.

I got a bad feeling about Ben.

"Researchers are now seeking what may soon be a new breakthrough against the appearance and long-term effects of cancer. Scientist Allen Stapher claims that the cells of cancer patients can be contained via a *simple* method previously not thought to have any remedial outcome for any known disease. By—" she continued, but John had heard all he needed to hear.

He was certain Ben was in the last throes of death.

Is it too late? Is he still alive?

John ran into the kitchen, through a short hall, up the stairs, and into Ben's room.

Ben was lying on a filthy, blood and shit-stained mattress inside a room more deplorable than the Georn City Dump.

The dirtiest clothes covered every inch of the floor, cups filled with mold cluttered every desk and nightstand, and plates fastened with stale, leftover food were crawling with maggots. The odors were worse than the sights. John's gag reflex was calling. His stomach was stirring, but his friend was in the center of it all.

He did not look even remotely well. In a sense, it did not even look like the Ben that had taken him in. He looked like he'd lost fifty pounds in the past couple of days. His milk-colored flesh was taut and the wrinkles on his face made him look like he was sixty or seventy instead of early thirties. The circles around his eyes were part black, part red. The eyes themselves had only moments of life left in them. He was dying.

John ran to his buddy's bedside and knelt down on a pillow on the floor. He grabbed Ben's hands and held them firmly but gently. "I'm here, Ben. I'm here, man."

Ben coughed. It sounded terrible, like he was drawing in a pool of phlegm.

He looked into John's eyes. "This day's come sooner than I thought. Time just flies by."

"Here, let me help you up out of this mess," John said and tried to lift his friend.

Ben reacted violently, swinging his arms, kicking out a leg, and twisting his brittle form. He fell back onto bed, cursing. "What the hell are you doing, *John? Goddamn!* I'm in enough pain as it is. I don't need you playing hero."

"You're laying in a cradle of filth!"

John reached down for another go. He didn't even make physical contact with him before Ben said, very calmly, "John. John, it's okay. I'm dying. It's not glamorous, and nothing will make it that way. Just leave me be. Please."

John's mind flashed back to the sight of Sarah Pouster

dangling from a rope.

Then his mind went back to Ben. How could he be thinking about a girl that no longer mattered when Ben was dying right in front of him?

"Ben—"

Ben held up a hand and offered the best smile he could manage. "I'm okay with it, my friend. I know you care about me. I know you want to pluck the cancer from my lungs, but dying is a part of life."

John teared up. "No!"

"Come on, I've made no contribution to this world, I didn't contribute to the arts, to peace, to solving world hunger. My life has no impact. The world is no worse off without me. No one will miss me."

"You're Ben Krambers! The best friend I've ever had. How would you feel if I was in your shoes?"

"How'd you feel if you woke up every day and regretted it? You hated yourself, your whole world, and didn't have a reason why?" He paused a moment to think, and then he continued with a more philosophical tone to his voice. "I'm not depressed anymore. Strangely, it seemed like the worse my cancer got, the better I felt emotionally. Spiritually. I felt *so* close to God when I first coughed up blood, like He was telling me, 'I'm here, I do exist.' I prayed to God my whole life, John. I know you don't know that, but I did. And do you know what I asked Him every time?"

John shook his head and held his friend's hand.

"I asked Him to end the pain. To stop me from hurting. He's doing that now. I can see everything so clearly."

Ben sat up and coughed horribly. Blood shot from his mouth. Despite the physical pain he was in, the smile never left his face.

"What is it?" John wiped away tears from his eyes.

"Swear to me that from today and until the end of your life, you will stop doing *this*—" Ben grabbed both of John's hands and clutched them very tightly. His fragile body twitched, jerked, and then regained composure. His breathing was now shallow; his stomach heaved, stopped, contracted, heaved, and stopped.

Ben finished, his voice barely above a whisper, "And start doing a lot more of *this*—" He suddenly *let go* of John's hands, fell back against the pillow, his stomach neither heaving nor contracting. His body went limp. Lifeless. Ben was gone.

He looked down at the young man he'd spent so much time with, recalling every experience he'd shared with him. He remembered throwing water balloons at him, hitting on girls with him, kayaking at Tappan Lake with him. He saw Ben smiling in the forefront of his mind and the way he used to sometimes snort when he laughed. Now his body had no remaining soul in it, just a shell without any goods. He would never get to eat his favorite meal again or meet a nice woman and get married. He didn't just die; he died prematurely, barely into his thirties. He had left no legacy, and had never gotten the chance to begin one. He never would.

His eyes were still open, looking skyward, his mouth partly open, a small grin still visible. John could not look away. Tears streamed down his cheeks. Sorrow was eating him from the inside. He wanted to wake Ben and tell him that everything would be okay by morning, but Ben was already on his way into God's greedy hands.

Slowly, effortlessly, a smile manifested on John's face as he thought about his friend's last words, his final piece of advice to a hopeless psychic. *You have to learn how to let go* was his message, a bit of wisdom that didn't pertain to John. The thought of the small sentence hurt him worse *and* began to heal the scarred tissue of his heart. His smile expanded. His cries turned into wails, but the pain turned into relief.

"I hear you, Ben, wherever you are. I know what you're saying, and you're right. I have a really hard time moving on. It's never been in my nature. I always fought the psychic side of myself. I truly did. But maybe I can use it for good. I'm no Jesus Christ, Buddha, or Gandhi, but I have to do the best with what I've got, and if that doesn't work, I shouldn't dwell on my failures. I can't win 'em all."

Letting out a long sigh, John wiped away his last remaining tears and covered Ben with the blanket. Afterward, he walked to the door and stopped, wanting to look back. He did so one last time. "I'll see you later, my friend. Be in peace in Heaven."

With that, he left the room.

He phoned the police and notified them of his friend's passing as soon as he got downstairs, and then relaxed on the sofa, staring blindly at the TV. No negative thoughts wrecked his mind. He actually felt at peace with himself.

CHAPTER SEVENTEEN

An ambulance and police cruiser pulled up to the curb right outside about five minutes later. John met two stout, lightly-dressed gentlemen at the door, who were equipped with a stretcher.

"He's upstairs. Straight at the end of the hall."

They rushed past him, anxious to get the job done. The cop, a large behemoth whose buttoned-shirt looked like it was going to burst, approached afterward. John stepped onto the porch to answer his questions.

Inquisitive neighbors looked out their windows or doors to see what was going on. Flashing police cruiser lights and the rumbling sound of the ambulance's diesel were drawing much unwanted attention.

"He died of cancer. I don't know how long he's had it. He didn't really tell me."

"Do you know the time of his departure, Mr. Rollings?" The officer's breath reeked of coffee.

John looked at his friend's cell phone. "Must've been around twenty minutes ago."

"Okay." The officer wrote something down on a notepad. "Thank you. Oh, here they come now." He looked over John's shoulder. John looked back and moved aside to give the two

EMTs space as they carried Ben's body through the living room and out the door, toward the ambulance.

"Do you need any more info?" John asked the cop.

"No, I think that will be all. Sorry for your loss." The cop offered him a grievous smile and walked back to his cruiser.

John watched the two coroners lift the stretcher into the back of the ambulance. The body beneath the sheet shifted with the rocky motion. This was farewell, a disconnection between friends. But, perhaps, from John's standpoint, maybe this was a new way of looking at the complexities of human life.

***

Later that night, Jennifer sat on her living room couch, her eyes burning, dry and strained. She looked through different versions of dictionaries and thesauruses, searching for the long word that began with the letter S. She had been looking ever since she had arrived home after dropping John off several hours before. Her head felt heavy, drained of focus and unable to evaluate any more information. The words in the books became fuzzy, jumbled incoherently together. The English language was looking more like a foreign language. Jennifer had the notion for some time to throw the books across the room and go to bed. Study tomorrow when she was refreshed, but she refused to give up. She only had what? Forty more pages to skim through?

God, kill me now.

She glanced up at the clock hanging over the mantel. 3:12 A.M. She never stayed up this late—not since she was a child at a slumber party.

She made the decision to call it a night after two more pages in Webster's Dictionary. Her tired hands wanted to drop the fat text. Her body wanted to fall back into the cushions of the living room couch.

Forcing herself to stay awake, she hammered forward. She had seen about every word in the English language starting with that single solitary letter, analyzed every meaning for a connection with individuality, and even had some choice possibilities written down.

She finished those last two pages, slid the books across the coffee table, and lay back on the sofa, drifting into the abyss of sleep almost instantly. She was too tired to go to bed or to reach to turn off the lamp.

It ate at her, screamed into her ear to keep hunting. She felt close to the word, as if she'd just passed it by. She rolled over on her side and wedged her face into a cushion. Something in her head kept saying *one more page, one more page.*

Her heart began to slow, and the real world started to recede away into nothingness.

I'm soooo tired.

One more page!!!

Sighing, Jennifer rolled around, reached for the closest thesaurus, and turned it to page 456. The first word was twelve letters long, started with an S, endorsed the relationship between one person, one goal, and almost eliminated her fatigue. She knew she had found the right one. No doubt.

"I got it!" Her eyes widened and she looked up, enthusiastic. She could not wait to tell John tomorrow, but first, now, sleep was calling her name again. Her brain shut off seconds later.

***

John woke up the following morning, confused. He didn't know where he was or how he'd gotten there. Charlie Steera's gravelly voice surprised him. "Hey, John, I just made some toast and eggs, if you want some. Get it while it's hot." He was standing in the doorway of the room, dressed in a blue, furry robe. "Oh, and I hope you like orange juice. That's all I've got."

This room, a bedroom, was unfamiliar, spacious, clean, and felt somehow neglected, as if it had not been used in some time. The cream-colored walls supported framed photos of Charlie and who he presumed to be his wife, a woman who looked strangely familiar. A parted closet revealed some clothes hanging inside: all women's clothes.

It started coming back to him. He had called the sheriff after the coroner and officer had left, seeking out another place to stay.

"Like I said last night, make yourself at home. You can stay as long as you like. I just gotta warn you though; I am a little eccentric as a roommate." He smiled and walked away, whistling.

For the first time in a long time, John lay back and thought about his financial situation. He only had what little cash Ben had given him days ago. Fifty Washingtons at most. Steera had never mentioned money, which he needed to get back on his feet.

He got up, stretched, yawned, moseyed on out of the bedroom, and entered the living room.

It was spotless—in immaculate condition—much the opposite of Ben's house.

John walked past a couch, a TV, and then entered the also well-kept kitchen. The tile floors were still wet from a recent mop, and gleaming. Crisp beams of sunshine blazed in through a window above the sink, making everything metal— the silverware, the table legs, the cabinet knobs, the sink itself—sparkle. But it didn't last. Like usual, some looming, dark-gray clouds covered the sun. Dreariness was in today's forecast—again.

Charlie was sitting at the table, eating eggs and reading an ad in the morning paper. He pointed to the stove, where plates were stacked with a variety of breakfast foods. "Help yourself."

John did. He put an egg, a piece of toast, and a piece of sausage on a nearby plate, and sat down with his acquaintance. There was already a fork on the table, as well as a full glass of orange juice.

"Thanks, Charlie, I really appreciate this." John dug right in.

"Yeah. I don't get company very often."

John thought about the bed and the room he'd been sleeping in.

Did I see a dress in that closet?

"Oh, no. Was that Mary's room I was sleeping in? I'm sorry if I—"

Charlie held up a hand. "No, it's okay. I wasn't going to deny you access to shelter, and I figured you might be low on money, too. I can throw a few bucks your way."

"No, you don't have to. Really, I—"

"Shhh. It would be my pleasure. At least until you get back on your feet."

John swallowed a wad of egg. "About that. Are we getting anything out of it? Since the government's now involved? I don't want to be doing this without *some* compensation, y'know?"

Charlie folded the paper neatly and set it down. "We will. In time. More, if we solve the mystery and destroy that terrible house. I hate it. It needs to be blown up or something. No, you'll get your compensation, some from the state and some from private funding. Some of the families of the victims who've either had someone die there or seriously maimed are putting up their own rewards to whoever finds a way to empty the clearing of that house. Everyone in Bellsville wants it gone. It's a bad local omen. A stain on the town." Steera looked thoughtfully into John's eyes. "John, do you think it is possible? To destroy it? And whatever's inside it?"

John looked him in the eyes and gulped down his entire glass of orange juice. He did not really want to answer. He didn't know. "I will give it my heart and soul trying to. I may lose both in the process."

Charlie took a last sip of coffee, exhaled loudly, and stood, reaching for his keys on the counter. "Well, I gotta go and run a couple of errands. Do you need anything while I'm out? From the grocery store?"

"Do you have any more orange juice?" he asked, tipping up his empty glass.

Steera pointed to the fridge. Nodded.

"Then I guess no, I don't." John finished off his breakfast.

"The bathroom is down this hall on the left. Towels and rags under the sink, in case you want to shower."

"Hey, are you going to be around Pokin's while you're out?"

"Yeah, I gotta pay a bill at the City Hall. It's close. Why? You need some clothes or something?"

"If you front me some money, yeah, I would like to get a couple outfits. I've been wearing these dirty rags for, like, a year now."

"Grab your coat, or whatever, and we'll go. I'll warm up the car. I'll be out there waiting." Steera left the room, then the house.

John set his dirty dishes in the sink. Afterward, he went back to his suite and put on his coat. Before he left, he reached into both his pockets and felt for two things: the wolfsbane and Ben's cell phone. Only the former remained. He pulled it from its cavern and examined it, just to make sure it was still vital and alive. The petals looked as bright as they had the other day, but he knew he would need to get more from Jennifer soon, just to be safe. If he wanted a chance to fend off D'kourikai during his ordinary life, there was nothing he needed more than this sacred, life-saving vegetation.

The phone, on the other hand, was nowhere to be found. He looked on every stand and dresser in the room but saw no sign of it. Had he forgotten it at Ben's? Had Charlie put it somewhere safe?

It didn't matter for the time being. He'd find it later. He wanted to escape the harsh reality of the world, the house on Mayberry Road, and D'kourikai by doing something a little simpler and enjoyable: shopping.

***

He jumped into Steera's warm, comfortable car a moment later. He buckled up, slipped on a Beanie, and held his hands in front of the heater. Charlie looked over at him, his fat hands at ten and two.

"Is Pokin's the only place you need to go?"

"Do you happen to know where my cell phone is? Did you see me with it when you picked me up last night?"

"No, I don't recall. You can use mine, if you'd like."

John shook his head. "I don't need it right now, but I will need to get a hold of Jennifer later. I need more wolfsbane."

Charlie gave him a funny look. "Wolfs—? What the hell is that?"

"It's a small flower. It's what keeps that monster that lives in that house from tracking me. The one I have won't last me too much longer."

"I see."

John looked out through the windshield. The roads were slushy, and the curbs, sidewalks and residential yards covered with snow. There was at least four inches in the shallow spots and about seven inches where it had accumulated. It had apparently snowed considerably through the night.

Kids dressed in snow-suits were everywhere, pulling sleds, throwing snowballs, laughing, building snowmen.

"All right." Steera jerked the stick into drive. The cabin jolted. "Let's make like a fetus and head out."

The vehicle squashed through some wet snow and drove down Yankee Street.

CHAPTER EIGHTEEN

Time passed too quickly for John that afternoon. He did not stay in the car during any of the sheriff's stops. He went in with him at Empire Foods, the Chester County Post Office, the City Municipal Building, and Family Dollar. He realized how much he missed being around people and being in normal environments where there were no astral projections, spontaneous predictions, or ghostly manifestations. He had almost forgotten what it was like being human. He had almost lost sight of himself during the past few weeks. But today— today was his vacation, a day to only be himself. He shopped at Pokin's, the second-hand clothing store, for nearly an hour, and purchased two shirts, two pairs of jeans, a package of underwear, and then he was done. They headed back to Steera's house at dusk.

The snow was really starting to fall when Steera pulled into the driveway twenty minutes before six. The roads were growing increasingly bad. Traffic had come to a standstill on certain local roadways. Luckily, the salt trucks were going up and down the many streets pretty consistently; the city wasn't taking any chances with the nasty weather. To John, as he stepped from the vehicle with a bag full of new clothes in hand, it felt like five below zero. The wind-chill made it feel like twenty below. John couldn't wait to get into Charlie's heated home.

Both men's faces flushed when they left the blistering cold behind and entered the warm house. John shut the door. He absentmindedly threw his bag of clothes on the chair. Steera turned on the light and tossed his keys onto the stand.

"Want a drink?" The sheriff made for the kitchen.

"No, I think I'm going to take a quick shower and try on my new clothes."

"Okay. While you're in there, I'll call your phone and listen for it, just in case it's around and just got misplaced. It could have fallen or slipped between a couple of cushions."

John headed to the bathroom through the dark halls. Once he found his way to the bathroom, he entered, turned on the lights, locked the door, and started the water in the bathtub. This room was no exception to the others.

It, like the rest of the house, was just as glamorous. It smelled good for a bathroom; the most dominant odor was that of scrubbing bubbles. The lights were sharp, well-placed, bright but not blinding. The mirror was without a mark and looked brand new. He went to it and looked at his reflection. He did not want this little interlude to be over with. His recent experiences had been stressful. Debilitating. It didn't even have many rewards, if any. He *still* saw Sarah in the mirror of regret, dangling, her tongue hanging out of her mouth. The worst was that sheet of paper stuck to her T-shirt. *The house has my soul.* It had been written in such innocent handwriting, by a hand of purity.

Would the image ever go away?

Would his guilt ever subside?

He shook his head and grabbed a towel. Before he undressed, a sudden knock sounded on the bathroom door.

"I thought you might like your new clothes." Charlie

smiled and handed him the Pokin's bag.

"Thanks," John replied, taking it and closing door. He set the bag down on the edge of the sink.

Steam billowed out of the shiny tub, slowly fogging up the mirror. The sound of the water was calming. He took off his clothes and stepped into the tub...forgetting a detail far more important than merely getting cleaned up:

The wolfsbane.

He remembered it right in the nick of time. Had he stepped forward an inch or two farther, its power would have be rendered ineffective by distance.

You almost just signed your own death warrant, dummy!

His heart beating normally again, he grabbed the wolfsbane, placed it on the lip of the tub, and commenced his shower.

The heat of the water against his cool flesh washed away not only dirt, but his wandering, negative thoughts. All accumulated waste, physical and emotional, spiraled down the thirsty silver drain. The persistent *shhhh* behind his head was soothing. It felt like a baptism, like he was being born again.

Approximately twenty minutes later, he shut off the faucet and stepped out into a steam-filled room where he patted himself dry with a towel. He dressed, grabbed the wolfsbane, and slid it into his pocket. Then he walked out the door.

He padded down the hall, first fast, then slower, then very slow. His stomach suddenly began to ache. His mind unexpectedly began to weigh heavily inside his cranium. The farther he got from the bathroom, the sicker he became.

He felt D'kourikai close to him again.

John came to an abrupt stop mid-hall, slowly turned, and looked back. He could not breathe, could barely move. He knew he'd certainly placed it in his pocket.

He reached into the jean pocket. His fingers felt a gross outcropping of tiny broken threads, and lastly...a huge *hole* at the base. There was a hole in his pocket—a hole that may well have led to his own demise.

He wished dearly that he had not been so cheap, that he had bought the jeans at JC Penny's, Macy's, Elder-Beerman's—anywhere besides Pokin's. By trying to save Steera a few bucks by going to a second-hand clothing store, he may have handed his soul over to the entity he feared more than anything. Stupidly, he knew Pokin's was well-known for selling defective clothes that ripped apart easily and sometimes had tears in them, but he never imagined it would cause this.

Now it was too late. D'kourikai was tracking him. He could feel its eyes spotting him, latching on to his location, coming through invisible barriers, space, and time.

Maybe it's not too late....

Was there any chance he could find his defensive weapon before D'kourikai found him?

And then he saw the wolfsbane, in the hallway about twenty feet from him. He started in a headlong sprint toward it, but was blocked by a stream of fire. The searing flames were not directed at him; they were directed at, and they obliterated, the wolfsbane. The surrounding carpet also got torched, blackened. Some of the paint on the walls peeled and curled. A faint, purple smoke dispersed from the blaze and spilled down the hall. A second later, it extinguished on its own.

He peered through the mist, trying to see what he was afraid of seeing. Slowly, like an illusion, he watched eyes appear within the confines of his reality—one, then two, then three, then four—all the way up to twenty-two. Its ceiling-bound body bubbled into physical form atop the bathroom door frame, its limbs emerged, and its hideous face appeared. D'kourikai was there, staring at him, into him.

"John Rollings." Its voice rumbled through the house.

"John? John! Are you all right?" Charlie Steera's voice called as he entered the room.

"Charlie, get out of here!" John cried.

"No!" Slime spewed from the entity's mouth. "He can stay. Maybe he will learn something. You humans learn, but your memories are short." It chuckled. "I should kill you right now for what you've done to me. The orange fluid that left *this* scar! You dare go back to her, I will see it. I will kill her and leave you wounded. You try to block my link to you and I will destroy everything that is yours. The time is here, John Rollings. It has finally arrived. I want you at my house tomorrow, before nightfall. You had *better* be there. If not, I can make your life a living hell for thousands of years. You will beg for death."

Then, without warning, the entity disappeared, along with the purple haze intruding the hallway. Neither man could move or speak. Steera gazed at his ruined carpet as if it was the greatest of his problems; John gazed at the ashes of the wolfsbane, knowing that this was finally the moment to stand or fall.

CHAPTER NINETEEN

The next day was a little warmer. Instead of snow, rain poured in a torrential shower, which washed away much of the accumulated snow. No sun showed itself. Horrific dark clouds covered the sky in a quilt of depression. Steera's car was no longer parked in the driveway. He'd left John a note on the kitchen table, which read: *Will meet up with you at the house. Take money on table for a cab.*

After reading the note, John sat on the couch and looked at his reflection in the turned-off television screen. He felt so many things and could not control any of his rogue thoughts. His stomach growled for food, but he was too tense to eat. He was so tired, his head felt like a bowling ball. He knew what he had to do, and remembered suddenly what Vaul had told him recently: *The sooner you do this, the sooner you get it over with.*

The phone on the nearby stand was standing tall on the charger. Everything inside him told him not to reach for it, but he did. His trembling fingers eventually pressed the right numbers, the ringing entered his ear, and the next thing he knew, he was waiting for a cab to come get him.

***

An hour later, John stood alone in the clearing, facing the

house, among several dead, torched soldiers—likely killed by D'kourikai—most of whom appearing to be no older than twenty-two. Their bodies were still smoldering, their skin black, their limbs stiff and bent at strange angles. There must have been twenty of them scattered about the field. Vaul was one. There were no survivors, no voices, no movement from anything or anybody. The place was a tomb, and the house was an instrument of death, run by the most despicable thing in any dimension. John was on his own, moments away from a supremely arduous confrontation.

He scanned the house from bottom to top: the strained, cracked foundation; the porch and its two paint-chipped posts; the front door that began to bubble outwardly before his very eyes; and the two topmost windows that moved vertically on their own, slanting at the inner corners like the brows of some enraged animal. The roof titled back, barely noticeably, and the porch roof curved into a little smile. Wood, plaster, and concrete were alive in a construction of evil. John just stood there, unmoved. He knew he was ready—*It* was ready—to now receive him. The door, which suddenly *exploded* into shards of splinters, confirmed this intuition.

He stepped forward. The walk seemed hours long, yet was so short he thought he had regressed time. His left foot met with the first step, his right on the second, and his left again at the top. He avoided the broken pieces of door, took a deep breath, and then entered the premises more reluctantly than a claustrophobe into a closet.

As soon as he was inside, there was a loud *ding*, and the doorway was suddenly blocked off by some large, foreign piece of matter. John turned and touched it. It felt like cloth in metallic form. Strong. Immovable. There was no way out of here.

***

John turned away from the sealed front door of the house and bumped into something, or someone. Grunting, startled, he looked up.

"Charlie." He breathed relief. "You scared me."

Charlie was standing on the first step up from the bottom of the staircase, Glock pistol in hand. He looked ready but stiff.

"What are you doing here?" John was confused.

"Waiting for you. Together, *we* will destroy this house. I want to *kill* the damn thing that lied to me about my wife."

John looked at the gun in Steera's hand. It looked useful enough, but probably wouldn't hurt D'kourikai at all. "What's the point of the weapon? How the hell did you even get in here with it?"

"I preoccupied *It.* If you keep your nemesis's mind on one thing, he may very well overlook something else."

John was surprised with his partner's contentious reasoning. "But how? How did you do it? What did you bait it with?"

Charlie smiled. "Y—"

His statement was lost when a loud, piercing shriek from the basement almost shattered both men's eardrums. They felt the high-pitched frequency in their bones. A minimal electrical charge shot into the bottoms of their feet and flowed up their legs. Steera stepped down and walked over toward the kitchen doorway, gun raised. John hurried over to him and threw a hand on his shoulder to stop him.

"You don't want to go down there, trust me. It's unnecessary to our objective. Upstairs is where the real problem awaits."

"I want to see it, John. I *gotta* see this for myself. Now, you can wait here for me, or come along. Whatever the hell that sound was, it sounded like something was being tortured to death. Didn't you feel the vibrations through the floorboards?"

John sighed. He was not about to fail his mission because Charlie was curious to see one of these beings face to face. And he was not about to let him go into the pitch black basement alone, either. Not when he knew exactly what was down there.

"We'll just take a look. If anything goes wrong, we'll come right up." Steera led the way through the doorway, through the dingy, disgusting old kitchen, and over to the open basement door.

The gun gripped firmly in his hands, Charlie removed a mag-light from his belt with his other hand and clicked it on. As they made their way down, both nearly slipped on slick goo covering the steps.

The large, direct beam illuminated the organic fluid, which bubbled in response to the light.

"Wow." Steera was intrigued. A look of childlike wonder appeared on his chubby face. "Incredible. Look what happens when I point my beam away from it."

"Yes," John sighed, "but we really need to concentrate here."

"Sorry." Charlie headed down the basement steps slowly, stepping over the green stuff, John right behind him. They maneuvered around some broken boards on the way.

Once at the bottom, Charlie stood in place and shined his beam around, panning from the far left corner to the far right. The entire room was doused in the olive-colored matter: the floor, rafters, walls, windows, and shelves. It seemed that wherever Steera aimed his light, there were more bubbly reflexes. "It's like something died."

John didn't like this. He knew it was the bodily fluid, or

blood, from the shrub that had almost ended him. Now something more powerful had ended it.

This hypothesis was confirmed a second later:

"What the hell is that thing!" Steera focused the light with a hand. The beam diffused and illuminated John's worst fears: the deceased and *mutilated* form of the massive carnivorous vegetation slumped over in the far corner. Thousands of thin branches and vines had been shredded apart. Petals were brown, blackened, smelling like rancid garlic. What John assumed was its head—a large, once-united spherical mass of tentacles—looked as though it had been blown apart by a bomb. Nothing moved except for the disembodied blood.

"John, was this that—that...thing?"

"Yeah. It almost killed me. That's why I didn't want to come down here."

Steera pointed the light at the plant's face and stared. It made him uneasy. "So, if this tried to kill you, then is it dead? It looks it. Smells it. What killed it? Could it have been the boss of this hellhole? D'kourikai?"

John, somehow, hadn't thought of D'kourikai as the cause of its death until Charlie mentioned it. It was highly possible.

"It could have been a number of unknown things that killed this—organism. I can't say for sure. But I don't want to stay to find out. We should not be down here now. You, Charlie, should not be here at all."

Steera took a few steps toward the deceased vegetation, astonished by its structure, its octopus-like tentacles.

"Charlie, this is the last place we want to be. Trust me."

"I know, I know. I just want to leave with evidence of the otherworldly." He removed a small plastic baggy from his pocket and bent over, reaching for a small, severed tentacle covered in green blood. His fingers met with the specimen. It was hard, slimy, and felt tingly against his flesh. Awe-struck, he looked back at John. "You wouldn't believe what this stuff feels like. It's—I can't explain how—" He trailed off.

John stood still, waiting, watching as Charlie dicked around.

"Do you have any idea what this could be worth in the scientific community?" Charlie continued, unaware of the faint, vague movement occurring in front of him.

"It might—" John began. He stopped speaking when he looked back at the sheriff and saw the substance floating out of the messy assemblage of damaged shrubbery.

"Watch out!" John pointed.

Steera fell backward. His head swung forward. He dropped the plastic baggy containing the small branch, but not his Glock. His eyes connected with a new, fresh, living entity neither man had ever laid eyes on before. It was not D'kourikai. It was a *pink gas*, or *smoke.* It swelled from the insides of its recent victim, through the gaps between the branches and leaves, searching for its next victim. And it found one in Charlie. Perhaps John, also.

"Ruuuuun!" John cried.

The sheriff didn't run; he didn't even move. He simply stared at it: a working, living, sentient being in the form of pink smoke. His eyes saw it, but his mind could not process it. His ears absorbed the soft, quiet whirling sound it made—like a small motor wrapped in cotton.

Slowly, it conformed to its own shape, from a dense, thick, compact blotch to a thin, transparent fog John could somewhat see through. It was oval at first, stretching apart at the molecular level, ready to devour the bizarre humanoid thing kneeling down a couple yards away.

Instead of running, Steera first aimed his gun at the thing, and then fired. Fire burst from the barrel, sending a bullet soaring through the pink mist and lodging into a wall behind it.

"What the hell are you doing? Don't provoke it!" John grabbed the beginning of the banister railing with his right hand, ready to flee.

Steera kept his gun raised, face streaming with sweat.

"Gently lower your gun, turn, and run my way as fast as you can. Until you run, take your moves light and slow."

The sheriff lowered his gun, but kept it in a tight grip.

The predator continued to expand, shifting fluidly from ovoid to rectangular to triangular to a star shape. Then a thin string of throbbing pink matter flew forward to wrap itself around Steera's throat, but he swung around and ran, catching up to John just in time to avoid contact.

The two men almost hindered each other's progress as they tried to run up the steps at the same time. Neither man looked back as they reached the kitchen and continued through into the living room.

"We gotta get outta here!" Panicked, Steera darted to the front door, which was sealed shut.

Next, he went to the window by the side wall and kicked it with all his strength. It did not budge.

"It's not going to let us leave!" John shouted. "Upstairs is our only way out of here!"

Steera didn't listen, wasn't hearing it. He aimed his gun at the glass and fired. The bullet bounced off it and fell to the floor, steaming and flattened. There was no damage at all to the glass.

John started upstairs, halted, and waited on the third step for Steera. "Come on, Charlie!"

Again, the stubborn cop aimed his piece at the window and fired. *Dink!* Another smoldering bullet fell to the floor, landing beside its casing.

"Come the fuck on! We're not getting out that way." John was almost screaming.

The smoke that drifted out of the spent shell was white at first...*then pink.* It intensified hastily and did not originate from the burned gunpowder; it was coming from the basement. The smoky phantom was resurfacing through the cracks in the floorboards, a gathering presence unwilling to let its victims go.

"Look!" John pointed. This time, his index finger quivered.

Steera rotated, looked down. Beads of sweat ran off his jawline. He had no time to aim or really move. All he could do was stand still, hope for the best, and look farther upward as the pink mist rose high into the air.

Steera's dead. There is no way he can escape, John thought.

John stood quietly on the staircase, out of ideas. He pictured the sheriff's obituary in the next week's paper, seeing him lying in the casket at the funeral home, and watching them lower him into the ground. That was if he was still in one piece after the uncertain nature of his demise.

Steera shut his eyes, puckered his face, and tensed all his muscles as the smoke finished gushing through the floorboards and filled almost a quarter of the small room.

The cloud changed into a variety of geometric shapes before settling on an exact replica of the person standing before it. The cloud-Steera grabbed the real one by the throat, overwhelming him with what appeared to be considerable force.

"Joooohn!" he screamed, reaching out for him.

I can't allow him to die, John thought, although he knew there was nothing he could do.

As John continued to watch Steera's clone choke the life

out of him, the imposter suddenly shifted back into a cloud of smoke and entered the gasping man's lungs. Steera looked like he was melting from the inside out. Blood poured out of every orifice, and the man began shaking in a violent seizure. John nearly threw up at the horrific sight.

Before John could speak or take another step forward, there was a sound coming from the nearest corner of the room. It sounded like a freight train flying through a narrow tunnel. It was the one and only D'kourikai.

Then the pink haze seemed to be pulled forcibly out of its partially digested victim. D'kourikai was inhaling it through its own expanded orifices, and even through its semitransparent flesh. John watched in disbelief. Surprisingly, Steera regained his breath, his bearings, and was released by the smoke milliseconds before passing out. He fell to the floor, wheezing, and looked up at the spectacle as it happened. The thing that had almost ended him was now being absorbed by another thing that should not have been.

A thin stream of pink turned into a thick stream of red. It was consumed swiftly, a colored rocket-fuel trail traveling in reverse. It started to screech and emit shrills of pain and panic similar to those of an injured whale. The remaining section transformed into a long cord-like shape and struggled desperately to grab hold of something, anything, but was unable to. The thrashing appendage almost knocked Steera's head off during its fight for survival. D'kourikai hung from the ceiling, mouth gaping, a vacuum cleaner sucking up a powdery ghost like it was everyday business. Pink matter continued to disappear. D'kourikai began to grow moderately in size.

Then, there was silence. Neither human so much as exhaled. Their eyes did not blink or move. The smoke entity was gone without a trace, replaced by the entity with twenty-two eyes, a more formidable opponent.

"Ah! I'm glad you both have come together. There is business between you humans yet to be hatched. You men didn't think I was going to let either of you be eaten by *that* unimportant creature, did you? I, instead, have eaten him. Just like your bodies consume nutrients, I can consume odors and liquids in ways you cannot grasp. Gaseous beings are lacking in intelligent matters. They go on instinct, nothing more. Kind of like the beings of *your* world. Except in your world, unimportant things matter."

John clenched his fists. He wanted to punch this thing. To end it.

Sensing the animosity, D'kourikai looked at him, smiling. "Minutes, my friend. Soon, we will finish our conflict. You will get your chance to fight me. I, however, will destroy you. And this planet. First, I must go upstairs and ready the battlefield. You must help out your friend here. He's okay now, I do believe. When your business is finished here, climb the stairs and pick the right door at the top, if you dare, for the entrance to the attic is sealed."

Slowly, the creature faded away until it disappeared wholly from both men's view. John unclenched his fists.

He glanced over at his downed companion, who was trying to get up on his own.

"No, wait. Here, I'll help you." John walked over, grabbed his hand, and pulled him to his feet. "Are you okay? I am so sorry that—"

Steera raised a hand. "No, just a few scratches, bumps and bruises. I'm okay."

"Are you sure? Let me see your—"

Charlie turned just far enough for John's eyes to catch sight of the *mark* on his upper back. A mark that nearly floored him. The bloodied image of a Grim Reaper. It was the one John had seen in a vision. It was the same one he'd seen inked on the man who'd killed Mary.

"What's wrong?" Charlie looked at him.

John reeled away. "Don't tell me it was you!"

Charlie looked as though he had no idea what John was talking about.

"You did it!" John backed away, shaking his head.

"Did what, John? What's the matter with you?" He came forward.

"Your wife wasn't just kidnapped and never found. *You killed her!* She sent me a message from the other side: that tattoo. It doesn't lie. You, all this time, have *lied* to me!" John backed against the wall. "It was you who broke into my room to steal the dream catcher, wasn't it?"

The new enemy smiled, grinned like an innocent child. "What's done is done, John. The past is gone. I did what I *had* to do nine years ago. That nagging *bitch got on my nerves!* She drove me *crazy.* I thought I loved her, at first. I wanted nothing but to be with her forever. But after marriage, everything went straight downhill. Saying 'I do' to her was like signing my soul over to the devil. She argued and bickered with me about everything under the sun. She *never* listened to me, *never* considered what I had to say, and *never* did anything but break my heart and make me feel like shit. My love turned to hate over time. I resented her. I wanted her to pay for hindering my entire existence. Murder was not really on my mind then. Why go to prison for the rest of my life? No, I let it go, until I saw her *cheating* on me!" Charlie continued coming forward; John, backward.

"She kissed some other bastard and never even saw me standing there across the street. *That was the last straw!* Well, we definitely fell apart after that. She wanted a divorce, but I wanted her dead, gone, never able to kiss any other *motherfucker* ever again. Still, I had few options. I could have gotten away with it. My being an officer of the law, I know ways to hide evidence, clean crime scenes. But I wasn't taking any chances....

"Then came the day when I chased that junkie into the woods out here. He ran into the clearing, where I went after him. I saw him sneak into this house. I took out my pistol and snuck in, myself. I barely began to enter before I saw him being eaten by the—that *thing* that was just in here. It left no trace of that man. Nobody would have ever found him, period. The monster—whatever you wanna call it—somehow knew my thoughts almost before I did. It could sense things it had no way of knowing. It knew how I felt about my wife and what my intentions were, so I made a deal with it. I would bring it a lock of hair from a young, undeveloped, male human soul, and it would wipe Mary off the face of the earth forever. Nobody remembers her, John. Nobody cares about that dirty slut. I was doing the world a favor by bringing her out here to this house after I drugged her coffee. She's gone, and so what? There are billions more to replace her. Don't fuss over one meaningless soul."

John's back was nearly embedded into the wall. Steera's face was in his, not an inch away. His eyes were filled with malice. "Are you going to hold it against me, John? Can't you just...forget? *One* measly person who made no contribution to the world. Can you let it go? We can still be friends."

John wanted to cry, but couldn't. This was the worst sort of betrayal. He'd trusted this man, and almost looked at him as a new friend, not somebody who, in a way, belonged to D'kourikai. And this foe was nothing compared to *It.*

"No! I will not let this go. You did something you have to pay for, Charlie! You killed your wife!"

Charlie looked down and chuckled.

He quickly stepped back, aimed his pistol at John's forehead. "I'm not paying for it. I did nothing wrong. Justice is in the eye of the beholder. Are you going to stop me? Knock me down? Arrest *me?*"

"No. You've done that to yourself."

Charlie laughed.

Steera's voice shaking, he said, "There is no God, John. No Heaven, no Hell. No Jesus going to save your soul. I'm just me aiming a pistol at your head."

"If you were going to shoot me, you would have done it already. I don't think you can."

"You have no idea what I'm capable of."

John gazed into Charlie's eyes. He peered behind them, beyond them. His mystical senses came to the forefront. He could see the immense sadness covering the surface of the sheriff's soul, and the forsaken, *loving* human hiding somewhere deep inside, below the pain, the fear, and the anger. He could hear Steera's subconscious mind screaming for help.

"You're not done yet, Charlie. It doesn't have to be over. There is no such thing as a point of no return."

"Oh, yes, there is. Don't try to save me. Don't try to psychoanalyze me. There's nothing you can say that I haven't said to myself before."

"That proves it. You're remorseful."

"Shut up!"

"You feel bad about what you did to her. To yourself."

The sheriff's face flushed red. The hand with which he held the gun trembled nervously.

"Give me the gun, man. You don't have to do this. You can get out before it's too late. This doesn't have to be the end. This can be the start of a new beginning."

Steera casually aimed the gun at John's chest, near his

heart. His finger wrapped around the trigger. Began to pull. John closed his eyes and clenched his teeth. But there was no bang, no flash...only an immense *crashing noise*, accompanied by the sound of glass particles scattering across the floor. The nearby window had exploded, and *another entity* dropped into the room.

Warf! Warf! Warf!

Lucky?!

John opened his eyes and looked over and down. Sure enough, it was his Doberman. Lucky stood menacingly beside Charlie, growling angrily.

By the time Steera swiveled around to aim his gun at the dog, it was already too late. Lucky did not go for the gun, or the leg, or the hand or arm; he went right for the kill. He leaped, knocked Charlie to the ground, and went gnawing for his throat. The gun fell. Saliva flew. The man covered himself with his arms to protect against the gnashing, hungry canines, which were not only sharp but hard as rocks. They managed to break some of the small bones in his hands.

"John! Call him off! Call him off!" Steera sounded more afraid now than he had moments ago.

John stood there, motionless, unable to move. *"Call him oooooff!"* Steera's scream became more desperate-sounding. Lucky plunged his slimy teeth into Steera's wrist. John could see the blood flow as a vein was severed.

"Ahhhh! Jesus Christ, help me! John, I'm sorry. I take it back. I'll do whatever it takes. Anything!"

John took a step forward, and then stopped, as if waiting for something. He had no idea what.

Do not help him, an unfamiliar voice spoke from deep within his mind. *Let this be.*

Lucky thrashed his head back and forth, along with Steera's bleeding arm. It was merely hanging by skin now, disconnected from tissue and muscle. It moved like cheap rubber.

With his capable hand, Steera reached for his Glock, which was on the floor beside him. He managed to grab it and aimed at the dog's squirming head.

Before he could pull the trigger, however, Lucky released his arm and went for his throat, this time severing major arteries, muscle and tissue. The blood was immediate, gushing from his throat and mouth. And then his body became lifeless. Charlie was dead.

Lucky let go of his neck. The sheriff's head thudded against the floor.

John patted Lucky's head as he stared in disbelief at the sheriff's bloody body. The worry, the panic, everything he had been feeling since entering this house, disappeared as he shifted his attention to the dog. "I never thought I'd see you again, buddy."

Warf! Warf!

"I don't think he could have been saved. Not like this. Not here, not now."

Warf! Lucky licked his paws.

"Are you okay?" John knelt down to examine his pet. There were no visible wounds through all the blood. "I missed you, boy. How in the hell did you get here? How did you know where to find me?" John almost expected a real response. A response came, swift and curtly, but it was not from Lucky. It came from upstairs, and was from a human female screaming.

Jennifer! Steera must have brought her.

John looked up past the dusty, battered old staircase, through the uneven railing, and to the top of the steps. "Ready to finish the job?" He glanced down at Lucky.

The dog barked.

"Okay. Let's clean this house once and for all."

Like that, they headed up the creaky wooden steps one-by-one, closing in on the Lion's Den.

CHAPTER TWENTY

At the top of the stairs, John stopped and looked up at where the attic door had been upon his last visit. Nothing was there. *Oh, what tricks does this bastard have up his sleeves?*

Lucky did a thorough pan of the area. The sunlight coming in through the windows was bright, despite the dark cloud cover outside, as if the windows looked into another world. The shadows created by this light seemed to twist and contort by themselves, as if even the very essence of things in this house had a life of their own.

A gust of wind came out of nowhere and ruffled John's shirt. He felt the chill of the sudden breeze beneath his skin.

D'kourikai....

He turned around and peered down the hall. It was shorter this time, only a fraction of the length it was before. There was no longer a room at the far end—only two doors on the right and one on the left.

Suppressing his fear—or trying to, more likely—John started forward, his sidekick clinging to his hip. Both doors were closed, their shells harboring any number of unnamable monstrosities behind them. The knobs stuck out like famished thorns. The rectangular frames seemed to bulge outward. Lucky sat right in front of the door to the left.

"Lucky? Is this the right door?"

Warf!

"Okay, I know you're right. I have faith in you." He petted his dog and stepped forward.

He knew that D'kourikai was standing on the other side of this door, waiting, expecting him. He turned the door knob. It turned easily in his hands. The door didn't just close, it *disappeared* behind them as they entered the room. John saw they were standing in the attic, right where the staircase once led up to it.

Hanging upside down from the ceiling, excited and ready to play, was D'kourikai. His figure was evident, visible, yet he cast absolutely no shadow on the floor under or above him.

And then he saw, suspended beside the monster, Jennifer, who was right-side up and dangling by her hair. Her nose was oozing snot, her eyes red from crying, her scalp pulled painfully taut. She looked traumatized and petrified—a mere instrument to lure in John Rollings.

"Jennifer! Oh my God!" He lunged toward her, but the creature swiped the air with a razor-sharp limb—a warning to stay where he was. "D'kourikai! If you harm her—"

"You'll what? Punish me?"

The monster chuckled. Parts of its body protruded, and a brownish-red limb ripped out from its lower body. It looked like a horse's leg without the skin. Attached to the end of it were half a dozen tiny fingers. They all pointed to John and wiggled.

"You are my key, John Rollings. Your soul has been prepped as a key. I will be able to wake Cthulhu again. From the depths of your Pacific he shall rise, and your little planet will be no more...at least not with your kind."

"Why me?" But then he remembered what Steera had done. Was the hair sample just to "prep" his soul for this moment? Is that how that event was somehow the origin of his psychic tendencies?

John looked passed the mounds of red, grotesque lumps of flesh on its torso, and at Jennifer, who was still bawling like a child in a dark well. Her arms were tensed, her fists clenched.

D'kourikai noticed his change in eye level and snickered. "Are you willing to give your life for this woman? Are you willing to hand your own soul over for hers? I will set her free for the price of your soul."

"Anything."

"No!" Jennifer blurted out, shaking her head. Despite her gnawing fear, she was not about to watch John sell his soul to this creature.

D'kourikai's mouth split open into three wicked smiles. Behind them, its teeth were of a distinctive shape, protruding from its green gums laterally. Its rancid breath smelled like toxic waste. The thing was just trying to intimidate him.

To John, it was actually becoming less and less frightening.

"It's okay," he mouthed to Jennifer, and then looked back up at his opponent. "Tell me what you want me to do. You let her go. Unharmed. And when she's safe, and out of this house, *miles* away from this house, I will comply."

Multicolored slime oozed from the monster's mouth. It splattered against the floorboards and burned a hole through them. "That's not how it works. You do for *me* first...then I free your girl."

John shook his head. "I'm giving you my eternal soul. If I'm so important to you, why can't you let my friend go first?"

D'kourikai paused, as if flustered by the question. "I'll let the dog leave."

227

"What?!"

"You dare question me! I should kill them both. How will I know you'll live up to *your* end of the bargain?"

"Because they mean more to me than my life."

"Fine. Both are free to go."

John looked from side to side. "How do you expect them to leave?"

"What, do you need a door, too? There are two windows!" It laughed, its many eyes blinking. "'Out of this house,' 'miles away'? Isn't that what you said? She can throw her fragile body out that window and an ambulance will take her as far away as you would like."

"Bastard."

Lucky had far less patience than his master. He growled and bolted forward, toward the disgusting monstrosity, intent on bringing it down from its place on the ceiling.

"Lucky, no!" John screamed.

D'kourikai continued to laugh as Lucky ran straight for him, legs kicking backward, mouth open, teeth gleaming, growl deepening. Jennifer watched closely, wondering if the dog was actually going to strike It unprepared.

Lucky closed the distance quickly, leapt up off his back legs, and was airborne, arching back his head so he could plunge his teeth into a dangling limb. But inches before contact, something happened, something awful. D'kourikai swiped the air with one of its limbs, and the dog's body split in half. The tail end flew left, and the front end flew right. Both ends slammed against the walls and thudded to the floor. Entrails scattered across the room. John looked down. Jennifer cried harder.

"Lucky...." Heartbroken, John ran over to his dying dog, knelt down, and cradled his head. A pool of blood saturated the floor around him.

"Why, Lucky, *why?* You were out of here! You were going to leave. You didn't have to save me. *Not this time!* Please don't die!"

John petted Lucky's head. "I love you, dear friend."

"Awwww. Such a pity. Now let's get down to business!"

Furious, John swung around, stood, and looked at the abomination. *"The hell with you! You killed my dog, you worthless son of a bitch!"*

"Watch the language, John. Temper, temper. Emotion blinds you foolish beings."

"And arrogance blinds *you!*" John clenched his fists.

"Are you mocking meeeee?!" It said, blinking its twenty-two eyes in a show of faux sadness. Its voice was so bassy it rattled the floorboards.

John didn't care anymore. He took back every bit of terror he'd bestowed upon this heap of aberrant biology. Sure, it was intelligent, manipulative, knew things by touch and feel, but its power was limited, too. It lacked simple emotional knowledge and had no apparent knack for even a hint of empathy. For as tough and menacing as it seemed before, D'kourikai now behaved like nothing more than a little boy.

"Let Jennifer go and I'm all yours."

"No! The animal attacked me. You've lost your privileges. She will be released *after* I have your soul."

John looked across its many eyes. "Then we have no deal. Besides, you could have killed us both by now and used me for what you need. What do you *really* want me to do? Get down on my knees and bow down to you?"

D'kourikai nodded and laughed. "Why, how did you know? I must have you drop to your knees."

"If I kneel, will you let her leave?"

D'kourikai laughed in response.

He knelt, not knowing what else to do. "Now what?"

"Lace your hands behind your back and tilt your head back as far as it will go."

"John, no!" Jennifer shook her head aggressively. "Don't do it!"

D'kourikai jerked Its head aside. As he did, the woman's mouth clamped shut. She tried to open it to speak again, but was unable. Her lips were firmly sealed.

"You don't know much about your girl, do you, John?"

John had no idea what It was talking about.

"This woman has known about you since you were a little boy. She has made a constant effort to get close to you. She has fallen in love with you. She hides secrets from you because of a faulty insecurity in her past. She's terrified you won't love her back, but she can't stay away from you. I just thought you might like to know that before you are parted from her forever. Oh, and she's ovulating, by the way, so I hope you wrapped it." D'kourikai chuckled.

"Shut the hell up."

"Aw, just playing. But now we must get down to business. I promise I will let her go. Now close your eyes and repeat after me."

John didn't have a choice. He shut them, praying D'kourikai lived up to his end of the bargain.

"Jussict-Vior-Morkten. Sechuist-Oppioriss-Miccee."

John repeated the words. He could already feel an unpleasant change in his body, down to the nerve and bone marrow.

"Tyrassian-Bore-Irpatini-Womlikor."

He repeated those words as well.

His heart started to beat erratically, and his nose began to leak blood. His brain felt like it was hemorrhaging. Dizziness emerged at once.

As the monster continued to speak his magic, another voice made its way into John's mind. The words were not verbal, but more like mental thoughts echoing across his remaining conscience with great clarity and strength. It was Jennifer's voice. She was speaking to him telepathically.

John, the word we were looking for in the warehouse...the word that was marked out, is Self-Sacrifice.

He tilted his head forward again and opened his eyes. Realization radiated bountifully from his face. His nose stopped bleeding. His headache went away. He felt better, as if he'd just taken a large dose of medicine. D'kourikai looked down at him with contempt, wondering why he had broken contact. "What are you doing?!"

John stood back up and shook his head. "No. I'm *not* just handing my life over to you."

"Ahh!" It quickly picked up on the psychical reception. "She speaks to you through mindful vibrations!"

Frustrated, the monster reached over and clutched Jennifer's arm so tightly that the bone inside made a loud *popping* sound. She let loose with an earsplitting scream. D'kourikai railed with uncontrollable laughter. "That's what you get for interrupting us!"

Getting an idea and suppressing it, John swiftly turned and ran toward the nearest window. By the time D'kourikai looked back at him, he broke it with his elbow. John picked up a big, sharp piece, put it against his throat, and turned back to the beast.

"You! You wouldn't!" Genuine worry exploded through D'kourikai's voice.

"You don't think so? I'll do it to save her. I'll do it just to spite you."

"If I let the bitch leave, will you drop the weapon?"

"Maybe."

"Maybe?!"

"I will."

D'kourikai looked closely at him, read him, and snickered. "I don't believe you. How do you like that? In every dimension I have ever visited, I have never come across a self-murdering life-form."

John dug it into his skin, drawing a thick bead of blood. His cheeks blushed. His neck muscles tensed up.

"Stop!" The beast made a STOP gesture with one of its limbs. Immediately, Jennifer fell to the floor, holding her broken arm with her left hand. Other than that, she was fine. Physically.

"There! I let her go. Now stop hurting yourself!"

A portion of the attic floorboards *cracked* and *exploded* down into the upstairs hallway below. A nice little square hole appeared for her dismissal. Before she left, she looked back up at John, thanking him via expression alone. He couldn't summon the courage to face her.

"Move along now!"

She stood and looked down into the opening. The broken boards were arranged together into a very poorly improvised, spur-of-the-moment staircase. It didn't look safe (nails and jagged lumber protruded from the woodwork), but it was far safer than the attic.

Jennifer retreated back to the standard world.

Now it was down to two. They watched each other carefully. John kept the broken piece of glass by his jugular, but lightened the pressure. It made D'kourikai nervous.

"You said you'd drop it. *Now drop it!*"

If I don't cut, it will win. I have to die like this in order to stop it.

He hesitated.

"You can't do it. Just as I'd thought."

An acute pain suddenly filled John's raised hand. It felt like spikes digging into his palm and descending down his wrist. The glass shard had turned molten and seeped through his very fingers. John looked down at it as it burned his skin and the tissue underneath. It hurt, but he somehow blocked it out. He didn't even wince.

D'kourikai's smile faded away. "Get down on your knees and finish your fate."

"You need me to freely offer my living soul?"

"Indeed."

"Instead, how about I sacrifice myself for all the souls you stole so that you could evolve? The poor Prestillion family? The soldiers who died prematurely? Or what about…"

"How will you do it? How will you sacrifice yourself for them? If you look back, you'd see that the glass is gone. You have no tool anywhere in this room with which to end your life."

"Oh, but you cannot force me to repeat your words back to you. You cannot make me go against my free will, can you?"

"With sheering pain, yes, I can. I can break you. The worst pain isn't physical, it's mental. The mind controls the body. So let's see what we can do."

D'kourikai blinked its twenty-two eyes. John stumbled backward, an aching throb filling every inch, every *millimeter,* of his brain. He had to react. He had to scream. This was something unexpected. Not once in his life had he felt so much discomfort, so much *pain.*

"A-ha! So you're not as strong as you thought you were, are you?"

I can't take much more of this.

"You can't take much more of this? Well how about *this*!"

233

Every nerve ending in his body felt like they had been ripped apart. His fingertips, his groin, his feet, his eyes, and his gums burned with an intensity greater than the sun. He could hardly stand. The pain was utterly unbearable.

Think of something peaceful, think of being somewhere else.

He thought of bunnies in a pasture, bunnies he had seen as a kid. The memory had always been pleasant.

D'kourikai *cringed.* It ingested the same memory, and it hurt *his* mind.

"What was *that?*" Its voice was uneven and permeated with extreme distress.

John noticed this and used it to his advantage. He opened his eyes and regained his balance. He gazed through his enemy, past Its nearly two-dozen eyes. Another memory resurfaced.

"Ouch! Mom! That hurt worse than the scratch!" John, at eight-years-old, with bright blonde hair and much lighter eyes than he had today, was sitting on the porch with his mother. This was when they lived in the house on Stiven Street, long before it had been torn down.

"It's okay, John." His mom gingerly cleaned his scraped knee with some alcohol. Her long, golden hair flowed in a slight breeze. "Just think, this burning actually *helps* the wound."

"It does? Really?"

She rubbed his head. "You're silly, Johnny." Her green eyes revealed the truth: she loved her son more than her own life.

D'kourikai stumbled backward across the ceiling, groaning. The memories John was recalling weren't *just* memories, they were times in his life that dearly meant something to him. They were memories he'd *forgotten* about, therefore things D'kourikai had no real way of seeing or knowing.

They were too beautiful and harmonious for It to bear.

Another thought popped up. Then another. And another. D'kourikai's body began to quiver, now in pain, not in glee. Yellow foam emerged from the corners of Its mouth. Its limbs swung around in radical circles. Its eyes bulged from their sockets and turned bright red, hemorrhaging.

And then the sunlight glistening through the only window intensified. The clouds were gone, unleashing a torrent of bright light. The floorboards began to steam. A rainbow of luxurious colors accompanied it, rapidly filling the room with heavenly character. The smell of roses appeared from somewhere, everywhere. D'kourikai grew increasingly alarmed. Something was happening, and neither being knew what, but it was in John's favor.

"What is this? What are you doing to me?!"

"Putting you in your place. You see, power comes with a price. What you may not know in your world is this: what goes around always comes around."

Ghostly but non-threatening shapes and shadows danced off every wall. They came at once, dozens of them, and were all of human origin. They were also the victims of D'kourikai, free from Its grip once and for all. Some swam around John, engulfing him in a sea of tranquility. Others swarmed the entity, overwhelming It, trapping It, attacking It. The apparitions ripped off Its limbs, which dissolved into nothingness once they were unattached from Its body. Its eyes exploded one after another, until It couldn't see at all. Black, horrible-smelling blood popped from every pore on Its body, and Its skin began to rip and tear apart.

"John Rollings!!"

In one last effort at settling the score, D'kourikai opened

Its mouth to full capacity and breathed fire at him. The flickering flames came forth fast. John had no time to duck or jump out of the way. He thought he was done for, and closed his eyes.

The heat was intense, but there was *no* contact. No unbearable pain or smell of burnt flesh. Still, his face was covered in sweat, and he reopened his eyes to see the last thing—*and person*—he expected to.

Sarah Pouster.

She was standing before him, her back to him, and her front blocking the onslaught of dragon breath. The flames did not affect her spirit, did not break through her glowing psyche. They were simply nullified by it.

John gazed over her head to watch D'kourikai try to ward off the spirits. They crowded around It, growing in number, not holding back, their expressions exhibiting supreme justice. Wounds continued to form. It continued to screech. The fireball, still protruding from Its mouth, soon went in reverse, back toward Its damaged body. As soon as it got near Its face, it engulfed It. Before It could retreat in any way, it was too late. D'kourikai exploded from the inside out. Sludge and slime flew everywhere: on the walls, rafters, windows, floor, John. The battle was over. D'kourikai was *dead.*

Things calmed down at once. Many of the spirits turned to orbs and flew out through window, where they floated up into the sky, free at last.

However, five others stayed behind: his mother, Mary, Sarah, and the Prestillions. They stood side by side, all smiling, all proud of John.

"You saved our souls." Mr. Prestillion's spirit glowed brightly. For the first time in centuries, he was happy again. Unchained. "You gave your life for us. We returned the favor, young man. I thank you!"

"Yes." His wife, a beautiful woman with long, fiery red hair, floated forward. Her hair floated with her. "Because of your divine choices, God has allowed us to restore a life just for you."

Sandra, their little daughter, a girl with pigtails, smiled at him with extreme generosity. "Yes, Mister, thank you!"

"You're welcome."

"We're sorry," Mr. Prestillion said, "but we can't stay. We must go now. Write about this experience, John. Share all your experiences with the world. God be with you."

The Prestillion Family's apparitions faded, then disappeared, gone into another realm, a better realm. A dimension of eternal serenity.

Mary, Charlie's murdered wife, floated forward and extended a transparent hand to her personal rescuer. John reached out and tried to grab it. There was no physical contact, but the hairs on his arm stood up.

"This is just the beginning, Mr. Rollings."

"Please, call me John."

She smiled. Her smile literally brightened the room. "You've done today what many people can't do their whole lives."

"What did I do exactly, Mary?"

"You brought a little bit of Heaven down to Earth. You destroyed a being stronger than something demonic. It was *all you*. We were only able to help after you'd done the hard part. If not for you, I, and several others, would still be trapped in darkness. I will see you later, my friend."

Like that, she was gone, too.

This time, Tamera, John's mother, came forward, her golden hair flowing. As she approached, tears filled John's eyes. His heart felt like it was on fire, but in a good way.

"John, my one and only son. You don't need my help any

longer. From here on out you got the rest of your life figured out. You may not know it right now, but you do."

"I won't be able to see you again, will I, Mom?"

She shook her head. "Not like you have been, but I will watch out for you from where I am. I won't ever leave you in spirit. Just because you don't see me with your eyes doesn't mean you can't see me. I will always be inside your heart. *Always.* I love you, Rock a bye Rollings."

He wanted to hug her so badly, but couldn't. It would have hurt him too much just to try. She disappeared before he could have, anyway.

"Good-bye, Mom."

Little Sarah Pouster approached him, the last remaining specter. She looked the way he remembered when she was alive, before she'd hanged herself. There was no remorse anywhere on her lucid face, no resentment, no bitterness. She actually looked very happy, despite what he thought he'd done to her.

"I'm okay, John. What I did was my choice, not yours. You made no mistake with me. You did not fail me. You have to let go of your guilt, or else you won't move on. You *know* that!"

"I do!" He wiped away some tears.

"Your friend Ben even tried to show you that, and still, you didn't really *hear* him. Knowing something and doing something are two different things. Today you did something that was more difficult than letting your remorse go. Why can't you do it?"

"Because I brought you to this house...your death is m..."

"John, if you can't let me go, I can't move on, either. We're all connected, even in death. So how about it? How about today you open your hands instead of clenching them together? I believe in you. You can do anything you want. Don't apologize to me, apologize to yourself. Let go. You freed hundreds of souls today, and now you can't save one, yours."

John wept quietly.

"You're close. Dig deep and say it. I forgive myself. I did nothing wrong to Sarah Pouster."

"I—I can't, Sarah."

"You can. You're just afraid. Just repeat these words, okay? I forgive me." There was no impatience in her voice.

"I—I forgive me."

"It was not my fault that Sarah died."

John cried harder.

Suddenly, the floor beneath him shook. The walls shuddered.

"It's—not my fault—"

"You're halfway there."

He searched himself for the words, for the lost region of self-liberation. It was there, confined and lonely all by itself, buried deep under loads of self-pity and ego. Inaccessible.

Using all his strength, he fought through himself to uncover it, to reveal it.

He couldn't.

"John, letting go is letting go, not forcing something away."

That's when his heart opened and he spoke: "It isn't my fault you died. It's not *my* fault. I did all I could and that's it. I forgive myself for blaming myself. I'm a good person and I love who I've become."

She smiled. The restraint on John's heart came unfastened. He was now free from himself. He could finally move on.

"Now I can go, too." Sarah began to dissolve away.

"Leave this house before it collapses. The portal is closing." She disappeared.

Particles of dust trickled down onto John's head. One of the overhead rafters cracked and came crashing down. The walls rumbled. Part of the ceiling caved in. He could see the sky, which was clear blue, all the dark clouds from earlier gone.

Ducking his head, John ran to the opening in the floor and began to climb down the hazardous-looking ladder. The split, conjoined two-by-fours constructing it rattled from side to side. His feet shifted hastily as he descended. Soon, the entire house shook violently, crumbling, smashing, and trembling like it was set above an active fault line. He lost his grip and was thrown down to the hallway below. Dazed but coherent, he got back up and went to the staircase. Using the banister for support, he helped himself down the racketing steps. The wall on his right cracked in a spider-web pattern. The brown-painted surface peeled upward. The unsettled dust became like clouds of poisonous smoke.

All John could think of was the front door at the bottom. It was no longer blocked but wide open. He could smell the fresh air, could see a strong breeze moving blades of grass. His legs moved faster and faster, going down from one step at a time, to two, to three. He almost tripped over himself twice, but when a loud *boom* rang out and the entire attic joined the upstairs hallway in a jumble of broken lumber and plaster, John was outside. Jennifer was standing by a tree several feet away, watching the house collapse. She did not see him come out, unscathed, running toward her.

"Jen! Jennifer!"

She broke her gaze and looked at him, astonished. *"John? Is it really you?"*

He wrapped his arms around her. She wrapped her

uninjured one around him and they held onto each other for several seconds. Neither believed they'd see each other again. John could hear her heart throb against his, her warm body press against his cool skin. Nothing could be better.

They looked back up at the disintegrating building. The roof had fallen in on itself, the windows all exploded simultaneously, and the brick exterior cracked in a thousand different places. It was *imploding*, turning in on itself. A small, whirling black sphere hovered motionlessly in the air, about where the attic once had been. *The portal.*

After several more minutes, there was nothing left but broken rubble strewn about the clearing.

John squeezed Jennifer's shoulder. "Let's go."

***

As they walked to the edge of the clearing, the sounds of sirens sounded in the distance, getting louder every second. Soon fire trucks were pulling into the clearing.

***

After making a series of statements at the police station about the house and the death of Sheriff Steera, John and Jennifer were both ready to call it a day. Officer Scranton was more than willing to give them both a ride to Jennifer's place.

Later that evening, over dinner, Jennifer looked deeply into John's eyes. "D'kourikai was right about one thing," she said. "I have fallen for you."

"What about your husband?" he said, pointing to her ring.

"I'm not married, John. Harold's my brother. It's all an act to keep guys at bay. I was afraid of getting hurt. I wear the band to keep them away. I've been waiting for someone like you, someone more like me." She squeezed him.

"Y'know, I think maybe we can make this work," John said with a smile.

"You're interested in me?" She looked into his dark eyes.

241

"Of course I am."

As they kissed for the first time, John heard what sounded like scratching at the door. And then a familiar bark *Wharf!*

"*Lucky?!*" He let Jennifer go and ran to the door. Lucky was burst into the house as soon as John opened the door. "I can't believe it! You're okay!"

He suddenly remembered what Mrs. Prestillion had told him. *"Because of your divine choices, God has allowed us to restore a life just for you."*

Lucky jumped on him, took him to the floor, and smothered his face with kisses. John burst out laughing. Jennifer stood there, smiling, spellbound. She could not believe a life had just been brought back from the dead, but it was so.

ABOUT THE AUTHOR

My name is Troy. My first, truest, and ultimate love is self-expression. I've been writing since the third grade, when our teacher made us write a story for class. That did it for me. I was hooked. I'm 33 now; I was 9 then. I've taken long breaks over the years, but I've never completely stopped, not even during my more depressed and doubtful times. Horror, science fiction, and fantasy are my fortes, though I have branched out: screenplays, poetry, philosophies, short stories, coming-of-age dramas, action, suspense ... you name it, I wrote it. One of the biggest contributors, I believe, to why I enjoy it so much, is because since childhood, I've had a crippling social anxiety disorder. When I'm around crowds or people I don't know, I freeze up, become very quiet. My heart pounds against my chest. I used to even black out and have panic attacks (very unpleasant experience, in case you never had one before). Don't know why I was always shy and awkward. Kids in school made it even worse. So, since I couldn't express myself verbally, I guess I used writing as a second form of communication. Strangely enough, I feel closer to God (or some divine force) whenever I have that spark of creativity. I feel like I'm closer to something larger than myself. It's actually like taking medicine.

So I guess this is where I say I start writing blogs to expose myself further out into the world. I don't care if I'm rich, or famous, or popular, or whatever. I just want my stories to reach people. To show people a side of myself I never could before, especially as a kid when I needed to most.

I want people to read something of mine and understand where I'm coming from, to take people on a journey into a brave new world they've never seen before. I want to share a part of my soul with humanity.